"I'm not after your house," Nate said.

"Then what are you after?" McKenna asked.

He took a step toward her, closing what little distance there'd been between them, his brown eyes blazing. Suddenly there wasn't enough air in the room. She felt a hitch in her chest, but she held her ground.

"I *am* jealous, all right?" Nate was within inches of her now, his gaze locked with hers. "Ever since I first saw you, you've been a thorn in my side. I wanted you. I want to ride off with you. I still want you and you're the last thing I need right now."

Before she could move or breathe or speak, his warm palm cupped her jaw and his mouth was on hers....

B.J. DANIELS

MATCHMAKING WITH A MISSION

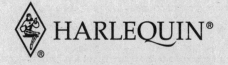

HARLEQUIN®

TORONTO • NEW YORK • LONDON
AMSTERDAM • PARIS • SYDNEY • HAMBURG
STOCKHOLM • ATHENS • TOKYO • MILAN • MADRID
PRAGUE • WARSAW • BUDAPEST • AUCKLAND

This one is for George "Clem" Clementson. A man who
understands the power of love and friendship.

ISBN-13: 978-0-373-88827-6
ISBN-10:   0-373-88827-9

MATCHMAKING WITH A MISSION

www.eHarlequin.com

Printed in U.S.A.

ABOUT THE AUTHOR

B.J. Daniels wrote her first book after a career as an award-winning newspaper journalist and author of thirty-seven published short stories. That first book, *Odd Man Out,* received a 4 ½-star review from *Romantic Times BOOKreveiws* magazine and went on to be nominated for Best Intrigue for that year. Since then she has won numerous awards, including a career achievement award for romantic suspense and many nominations and awards for best book.

Daniels lives in Montana with her husband, Parker, and two springer spaniels, Spot and Jem. When she isn't writing, she snowboards, camps, boats and plays tennis. Daniels is a member of Mystery Writers of America, Sisters in Crime, Thriller Writers, Kiss of Death and Romance Writers of America.

To contact her, write B.J. Daniels, P.O. Box 1173, Malta, MT 59538 or e-mail her at bjdaniels@mtintouch.net. Check out her Web page at www.bjdaniels.com.

Books by B.J. Daniels

CAST OF CHARACTERS

McKenna Bailey—The cowgirl had always been drawn to the house—and the boy she'd seen in the third-story window.

Nate Dempsey—Had he come back to Whitehorse looking for revenge and redemption? Or was it always about the girl?

Johnny Dempsey—If he could be found, he would hold all the answers.

Flynn Garrett—He'd come back to Whitehorse knowing he was going to have to make a choice.

Roy Vaughn—What had happened to the bully who'd terrorized the boys at Harper House?

Frank Merkel—He wasn't afraid of a bunch of bad boys or some blood oath that called for killing anyone who'd ever worked at Harper House.

Rosemarie Blackmore—She knew more than she was telling about Harper House and what went on there years ago—and it could get her killed.

Ethel Winthrop—She tried to warn people about what had gone on at that house, but no one would listen.

Chapter One

He'd known where she was for almost two weeks. He'd been watching her house, watching her. He just hadn't felt a need to do anything about it.

Until now. Fate had forced his hand. He didn't have much time left. He had to use it wisely. Take care of all those loose ends in his life.

As he pried at the flimsy lock on the side window he thought about how he had loved her. Idolized her. Thought she was the most beautiful woman he'd ever seen.

Unfortunately she hadn't felt the same way about him.

The lock snapped with a soft pop. He froze, listening even though he knew she wouldn't have heard it. Usually by this time of the night she'd finished off enough cheap wine that she would be dead to the world.

Dead to the world. He liked that. He'd been dead to the world thanks to her.

He'd planned this for so long and yet he felt uneasy, a little thrown by the fact that he'd had to break in tonight. All the other nights, she'd forgotten to lock up. Why tonight, of all nights, did she have to remember to lock the damn doors?

A few days ago he'd waited in the overgrown shrubs outside, watching her shadow move behind the sheer curtains in the living room to turn off the television before she stumbled down the hall to bed.

When he'd been sure she'd passed out, he'd slipped inside the house, wanting to take a look around, to know the layout of the house. Not good to bump into something and wake her up on the night he planned to finally finish it.

So he'd poked around, looking into her things, seeing how she'd been doing since he'd last seen her. He'd made a point of testing to see just how deep a sleeper she was. He couldn't have her screaming her head off when the time came, now could he?

For some reason tonight, though, she'd locked the doors. He tried not to let that worry him. But he was superstitious about crap like that. It was her fault. She'd put all that hocus-pocus stuff in his head, her and her horoscopes, palm readings and psychic phone calls. She wouldn't cross the street without checking to make sure her stars were aligned.

Except when she was drunk. Then she threw caution to the wind. He hated to think he was a lot like her that way. Except he didn't have to be drunk.

So, as much as he hated it, he was leery as he hoisted himself up and over the windowsill to drop into the bathroom tub. He landed with a thud and froze to listen.

Maybe she'd remembered to lock the front door because her horoscope told her that she should be more careful today. Or she could have spotted him watching the house, he supposed. But wouldn't it also be possible, given the connection between them, that she'd sensed he was here?

He liked the latter explanation the best. That would mean that she had occasionally thought of him, wondered what had happened to him.

A shell-shaped night-light next to the sink made the bathroom glow pink. She'd done the whole place in a tropical motif. The shower curtain was plastic with huge palm trees. What the hell had she been thinking? As far as he could tell, she'd been landlocked all her life and never even seen an ocean, let alone a real palm tree.

He wasn't sure why, but it made him even more angry with her, this pretending she lived in a beach house. Did she also pretend he'd never existed?

The shower curtain made a soft swishing sound as he brushed against it. Again he froze and listened. A breeze wafted in with the smell of the river.

He thought he heard a noise from the bedroom. The creak of bedsprings as she rolled over. Or got up to come find out what the noise had been in the bathroom. Had she bought herself a gun?

He waited behind the shower curtain, hidden by the fake palms. *I'm right here. Right here. Just waiting for you.*

It surprised him how nervous he was about seeing her again. He'd anticipated this moment for so long he'd expected to be excited. But as he drew the switchblade from his pocket, his fingers were slick with sweat. He wiped them on his jeans and blamed the hot, humid night.

It reminded him of other hot nights, lying in bed, afraid he wouldn't live until morning. The only thing that had kept him going was imagining this day, the day he found her and made her pay for what she'd done to him.

He wanted her to know that kind of fear before this night was over. He glanced at his watch in the glow of the shell night-light. He had plenty of time before her husband came home.

She'd married some guy who worked the graveyard shift as a night watchman. The irony of that didn't escape him as he got tired of waiting in the bathtub and peered around the edge of the shower curtain.

No movement out in the hall. No sound coming from the vicinity of the bedroom. Gently he slid the curtain aside to step out onto the mermaid-shaped shag rug.

He felt hatred bubble up as he noticed she'd bought herself a pretty new mirror since he was here just a few days ago. The mirror was framed in seashells, and it was all he could do not to smash it on the tile floor.

It wasn't the mirror. Or even the stupid seashore stuff. It was that she'd done just fine without him. Better than fine once she'd dumped him.

The realization was like acid inside him. It ate away at the hope that she'd missed him. That she'd been sorry she'd left him.

He thought of the seven-year-old boy he'd been. He could smell the dust her car tires had thrown up as she'd torn across the dirt lot of the filling station. He'd run out of the restroom, thinking she hadn't realized he wasn't in the car, and had called after her. Running, tears streaming down his dirt-streaked face, until he'd stumbled and fallen and lain bawling his heart out as her car had grown smaller and smaller on the two-lane highway in the middle of nowhere.

The memory jarred him into motion. Stepping

through the bathroom doorway, he stopped to wait for his eyes to adjust. Her bedroom door was closed. That was odd. It had been open when he'd been here a few nights before.

Worry knifed through him. The hallway was lit by another shell night-light. The cramped space smelled of stale beer and old cigarette smoke.

He inched down the hall, anticipation thrumming in his veins. At the door, he stopped, suddenly worried what he would do if for some reason she'd locked it.

His hand shook as he reached out and took the knob in his damp fingers. He closed his eyes, knowing it couldn't end here, with him locked out of her room, and that it would end very badly if he had to break down the door. She would be able to call the police before he could get to her. He should have cut the phone lines, he realized now.

The knob turned in his hand.

He slumped against the doorjamb for a moment, his relief so intense it made him light-headed. He was sweating hard now, his T-shirt sticking to his skin, and yet he felt a chill as he looked into her bedroom.

The bed was one of those California kings he'd heard about—and damned near as big as the bedroom. He could make out a small form under the covers. Another one of those stupid shell night-lights glowed from a corner of the room.

He stepped in. The only sound was her drunken snores. She was curled on her side, her back to him on the edge of the bed farthest from him. All he could see was the back of her head on the pillow. Her hair was darker than he remembered it. He realized she probably dyed it because she could be getting gray by now.

It finally struck him: he was going to come face-to-face with the mother who had abandoned him at a gas station twenty-four years ago.

A memory blindsided him. A memory so sweet it made his teeth ache. The two of them sitting on the couch watching her favorite soap opera. A commercial came on for hair color. Him telling her she would look beautiful no matter what color her hair was, even gray. And her smiling over at him, tears in her eyes as she kissed his cheek and pulled him into her arms for a hug.

She'd held him so tightly he couldn't breathe. But he hadn't complained. It was the last time he remembered her touching him.

He crept around the perimeter of the bed, feeling as if he were floating. It all felt so surreal now that he was finally here, finally ready.

She stirred and he froze. She let out a sigh and drifted off again. He edged closer until he was standing over her.

He couldn't see her face. Not the way he wanted

to. He knew he was going to have to turn on the lamp beside her bed. He wanted to look into her eyes—and have her look into his. He wanted her to know.

As he turned on the lamp, his fingers brushed the stack of old magazines next to the bed. The magazines toppled over, hitting the floor with a whoosh that startled him as much as the brightness of the lamp as it came on.

She jerked up in bed onto one elbow, blinking against the brightness of the light.

He could see that for a moment she thought he was her husband. She'd aged. It shouldn't have shocked him. But she'd been only twenty-three when she'd left him at that filling station in Montana. She wasn't even fifty, and yet she looked a lot older.

He'd always wondered if she'd grieved over what she'd done. Her life's road map was etched unkindly in her face, but he knew that the very worst she'd had wasn't even close to what he'd been through.

She blinked, that moment of mistakenly taking him for her husband turning to confusion, then fear. Her mouth started to open as she clutched the sheet to her throat.

"Don't scream," he said and touched the knife in his hand, the blade leaping out to catch the light. "Don't you dare scream."

Surprisingly, she didn't. Only a small sound came out of her as her eyes met his and he saw the recognition.

That should have given him some satisfaction. She knew him even after all these years.

He used to have this dream that she would fall to her knees and beg his forgiveness. He'd always wanted to believe that she'd come back for him but it had been too late. He'd thought about her searching for him for years, her life as miserable as his had been because of what she'd done.

The dream popped like a soap bubble when she opened her mouth again. "So you found me." Her voice was rough from years of cigarettes and late-night boozing, bad men and barrooms.

"So what now?" she asked with a shake of her head. Her eyes flicked to the switchblade in his hand and something came over her face. A hardness that he now remembered from when he was a boy.

What he saw in her eyes was not the remorse he'd hoped for. No sorrow. No guilt. Not even fear anymore. Her gaze was challenging. As if telling him he didn't have what it would take to kill her.

"You think I haven't always known that you'd turn up one day?" she said as she sat up in the bed and reached for her cigarettes and lighter on the nightstand. She lit a cigarette and took a deep drag.

He stared at her. He'd often wondered if that day at the gas station she'd looked in her rearview mirror. Now he knew that answer. She hadn't looked back. Not even a glance. He guessed he'd always known that.

"Don't you want to know what happened to me?" A seven-year-old boy abandoned like that. He wanted to tell her about the man who'd picked him up and eventually dumped him just the way she had. Dumped him at a place with an innocuous name: Harper House.

He and the others, though, they'd called it Hell House.

Her eyes narrowed at the question, cigarette smoke curling around her. "What? You want to swap horror stories?" She let out a laugh that turned into a cough. "I could tell you stories that would make your hair curl."

She must have seen his hurt. "Hoping for a heartwarming reunion, were you?" She flicked another glance at the knife. "Or were you thinking you could get money out of me?" She let out another laugh. "Sorry, but you're going to be disappointed on both counts."

He shook his head. What had he expected from a woman who'd abandoned her only child the way she had? "Just tell me *why*."

She blew out a cloud of smoke. "*Why?* That's it? That's all you want to know?" She gave a drunken nod of her head. "Because I knew you were going to turn out just like your father. And—you know what?—I was right. I should have gotten rid of you like he wanted me to before you were even born."

He'd wanted to make her suffer, but in the end it had all gone too quickly. Still, he'd thought that once she was dead he would feel some release, some measure of peace. Instead he felt empty and angry, just as he had for years.

He'd just finished her when he heard someone coming in the front door of the house. The husband coming home early.

It often amazed him the way things happened—as if they were meant to be. He waited until the husband came down the hall. Killing him was too easy.

Taking the credit cards and checkbooks, along with what cash he found in the house, proved a little more satisfying.

As he climbed out her bathroom window after smashing the shell-framed mirror to sand, he walked to his pickup parked down the block and told himself he wouldn't find the peace he'd spent his life searching for until everyone who'd hurt him was dead.

He didn't need to check the map. He knew the way to Whitehorse, Montana. Unlike his mother, he'd spent more time there than what it took to put five dollars worth of gas into the tank and drive away.

He'd spent the worst years of his life just outside of that town. And now he was going back for the first and last reunion of Harper House. It would end where it started.

But first there were a couple of stops he needed to make along the way. There couldn't be any loose ends.

He checked to make sure he had the switch-blade he'd cleaned on her tropical-print sheets and told himself it had been destined to end this way.

Still, as he drove away it nagged at him. What kind of mother just drove off and left her son beside the road? He eased his pain with the thought that the babies must have been switched at the hospital. His real mother was out there somewhere. She'd spent her life looking for him, feeling that something was missing.

He felt a little better as he drove west toward Montana. By the time he reached the border he'd convinced himself that he'd been stolen from his real parents—a mother who loved him and a father who would never have run out on him.

He *had* to believe that. He couldn't accept that he'd killed his own mother. Otherwise, it might be true what she'd said about him being like his father.

Chapter Two

McKenna Bailey rode her horse out across the rolling prairie, leaving behind Old Town White-horse. The grass was tall and green, the sky a crystalline blue with small white clouds floating along on the afternoon breeze.

She breathed in the warm air, wondering how she could have stayed away from here as long as she had.

The ride south toward the Missouri Breaks was one she knew well. Even before she was able to sit alone in a saddle she'd ridden hugging the saddle horn, in front of her older sister Eve.

Lately she'd felt antsy and unsure about what she wanted to do with her life. So she'd come home to the one place that always filled her with a sense of peace. But since she'd been home she'd realized this was where she belonged—not opening her own veterinarian clinic as she'd planned since she was twelve because she loved animals. Especially horses.

On impulse, she angled her horse to the east and watched the structures rise up out of the horizon ahead, an idea taking shape.

The barn came into sight first, a large weathered building with a cupola on top and a rusted weather vane in the shape of a horse. As she drew closer she heard the eerie moaning sound of the weather vane as it rotated restlessly in the breeze. It was a sound she remembered from when she used to sneak over here as a young girl.

As she rode closer, the house came into view. The old Harper place. She felt a rush of adrenaline she'd never been able to explain. Something about the house had always drawn her—even against her father's strict orders that she and her sisters stay far away from the place.

Chester Bailey had said the property was dangerous. Something about it being in disrepair, old septic tanks and uncovered abandoned wells. Things horses and kids could get hurt in.

McKenna had never gone too close, stopping at the weathered jack fence to look at the house. The structure was three stories, a large old ranch house with a dormer window at each end. An old wooden staircase angled down from the third floor at the back. A wide screened-in porch ran the width of the house in the front.

Her gaze just naturally went to the third-floor window where she'd seen the boy. She'd been six. He'd looked a couple years older. She had never forgotten him. He'd disappeared almost at once, and an old woman had come out and run her off.

As she stared up at the window now, sunlight glinting off the dirty glass, she wondered what had happened to that sad-looking boy.

Whoever had lived there moved shortly after that, and the house had been occupied by Ellis Harper, an ornery old man who threatened anyone who came near. He kept a shotgun loaded with buckshot by the backdoor.

McKenna had heard stories about the house. Some of the kids at the one-room school she'd attended in Old Town Whitehorse had whispered that Ellis Harper stole young children and kept them locked up in the house. Why else wouldn't he let anyone come around? For years there'd been stories of ghosts and strange noises coming from the house.

McKenna didn't believe in ghosts. Even if she had, she doubted it would have changed the way she felt about this place. She'd ridden over here even when Ellis Harper had been alive, but she'd never gone farther than the fence. Too many times she'd seen his dark silhouette through the screen door, the shotgun in his hands.

As she sat on her horse at the fence as she'd done as a child, she realized she'd always been so captivated by the house and its occupants that she'd never noticed the land around it.

The breeze rustled the new leaves on the copse of cottonwoods that snaked along the sides of the creek and through the rolling grasslands. Good pastureland and, unless she was mistaken, about forty acres worth. There were several old out-buildings a good ways from the house, and then the big old barn and a half dozen old pieces of farm machinery rusting in the tall weeds.

While the idea had come to her in a flash, she knew it had been in the back of her mind for years. She had always been meant to buy Harper House and the land around it.

She just hadn't known until that moment what she planned to do with it.

NATE DEMPSEY SENSED someone watching the house and looked out in surprise to see a woman astride a paint horse just on the other side of the fence. He quickly stepped back from the filthy second-floor window, although he doubted she could have seen him. Only a little of the June sun pierced the dirty glass to glow on the dust-coated floor at his feet as he waited a few heartbeats before he looked out again.

The place was so isolated he hadn't expected

to see another soul. Like the front yard, the dirt road in was waist-high with weeds. When he'd broken the lock on the back door, he'd had to kick aside a pile of rotten leaves that had blown in last fall.

As he sneaked a look, he saw that she was still there, staring at the house in a way that unnerved him. He shielded his eyes from the glare of the sun off the dirty window and studied her, taking in her head of long blond hair that feathered out in the breeze from under her Western straw hat.

She wore a tan canvas jacket, jeans and boots. But it was the way she sat astride the brown-and-white horse that nudged the memory.

He felt a chill as he realized he'd seen her before. In that very spot. She'd just been a kid then. A kid on a pretty paint horse. Not this one—the markings were different. Anyway, it couldn't have been the same horse, not considering the last time he had seen her had been more than twenty years ago. That horse would be dead by now.

His mind argued it probably wasn't even the same girl. But he knew better. It was the way she sat on the horse, so at home in a saddle and secure in her world on the other side of that fence.

To the boy he'd been, she and her horse had represented freedom, a freedom he knew he would never have—even after he escaped this house.

Nate saw her shift in the saddle, and for a moment he feared she planned to dismount and come toward the house. With Ellis Harper in his grave, there would be little to keep her away.

To his relief, she reined her horse around and rode back the way she'd come.

As he watched her ride off he thought about the way she'd stared at the house—today and years ago. While the smartest thing she could do was stay clear of this house, he had a feeling she'd be back.

Finding out her name should prove easy since he figured she must live close by. As for her interest in Harper House… He would just have to make sure it didn't become a problem.

"I THOUGHT WE'D ALREADY discussed this?"

McKenna Bailey looked up from the real-estate section of the newspaper the next morning as her sister Eve set down a platter of pancakes.

"You don't need to buy a place," Eve Bailey said as she pulled up a chair and helped herself to a half dozen of the small pancakes she'd made. "You can live in this one and use as much of the land as you need for this horse ranch you want to start."

McKenna watched her older sister slather the cakes with butter before drowning them with chokecherry syrup. "Are you nervous about getting married next month?" she asked, motioning at Eve's plate.

Eve looked up, a forkful of pancakes on the way to her mouth. "No, I'm just *hungry.*"

"Right," McKenna said. "Like the way you've suddenly started holding your fork with your *left* hand?"

Eve looked down at the fork, then at the engagement ring on her left hand and smiled. "It *is* beautiful, isn't it?"

McKenna nodded, smiling at her older sister across the table, the same table they'd shared since they were kids.

"I am doing the right thing, aren't I, marrying Carter?" Eve asked with a groan as she pushed her plate away.

"You love Carter and he loves you," McKenna said. "Be happy. And *eat.*"

"You'd tell me if you thought I was making a mistake?"

McKenna nodded, smiling. Carter Jackson had broken her sister's heart back in high school when he'd married someone else. That marriage had been a disaster, ending in divorce. McKenna had no doubt that Carter loved her sister as much as Eve loved him. For months the poor man had been trying to win Eve back; finally at Christmas he'd asked her to marry him. The Fourth of July wedding was just weeks away now.

Eve pulled her plate back in front of her and picked up her fork. "I really *am* hungry."

McKenna laughed and went back to studying the real-estate section of the *Milk River Examiner.* But none of the houses interested her. There was only one place she wanted, and even though she'd heard the owner had died recently, she didn't see it listed. Maybe it was too soon.

"I'm serious," Eve said between bites. "Just live in this house. With Mom and Loren living in Florida, it's just going to be sitting empty."

McKenna looked around the familiar kitchen. So many memories. "Dad doesn't want the house?"

Eve shook her head. "He's moved in with Susie, and they're running her Hi-Line Café. He seems… happy."

"Do you know if anyone has bought the old Harper place?" McKenna asked.

"You can't be serious." Eve was staring at her, her mouth open. "Harper House?"

"Did you leave me any pancakes?" their younger sister, Faith, asked as she padded into the room in a pair of pajama bottoms and a T-shirt and plopped down at her chair. "What about Harper House?"

Eve shoved the platter of pancakes toward Faith without a word and gave McKenna a warning look.

"Is anyone going to answer me?" Faith asked

as she picked up a pancake in her fingers, rolled it up and took a bite. She looked from Eve to McKenna and back. "Are you guys fighting?"

"No," Eve said quickly. "I was just telling McKenna that she could have this house," she said with a warning shake of her head at McKenna. There was a rule: no fighting, especially when Faith was around.

The youngest of the three girls, Faith had taken their parents' divorce hard and their mother's marriage to Loren Jackson even harder. Because of that, both Eve and McKenna had tried to shelter their younger sister. Which meant not upsetting her this morning with any problems between the two of them.

"It would be nice if someone lived here and took care of the place," Eve said.

"Not me," Faith said and helped herself to another pancake.

"It's our *family* ranch," Eve said.

"That's why I want a place of my own close to here," McKenna said.

Faith shot her a surprised look. "Are you really staying around here?" Since high school graduation she and Faith had come home only for holidays and summer vacation from college.

"I think I'm ready to settle down, and this area is home," McKenna said.

Faith groaned. "Well, I'm not coming back

here to live," she said, getting up to pad over to the kitchen counter to pour herself a cup of coffee.

"I don't want to see this house fall into neglect, either," McKenna told Eve. "But I want my own place. This house is…"

"Mom's and Dad's," Faith said as she came back to the table with her coffee, tears in her eyes. "And now, with Mom and Dad divorced and her married to Loren and living in Florida, it just feels too weird being here."

McKenna knew that Eve had come over this morning from her house down the road to cook breakfast in an attempt to make things more normal for her and Faith. Especially Faith.

"Where are you and Carter going to live after you're married?" McKenna asked Eve.

"My house." Eve had moved into what used to be their grandmother's house when Grandma Nina Mae Cross had gone into the rest home. "We're going to run cattle on the ranch, as always. It's what put us all through college. It's our heritage."

Faith shot McKenna a look that she knew only too well. *Here goes Eve, off on one of her legacy speeches.*

The ranch had always been intended for the three of them. Since Eve had returned she'd been running the place and sending both McKenna and Faith a share of the profits.

"So what happens to this house?" Faith asked, clearly trying to cut Eve off before she got started.

"I guess if the two of you don't want it, the house will just sit empty," Eve said, giving McKenna one of her meaningful big-sister looks.

"That's awful," Faith said. "Someone should live here."

McKenna watched her little sister run a hand along the worn tabletop and smiled. She didn't know what it was about this part of Montana, but it always seemed to bring them back. She'd watched friends leave for college, swearing they were glad to be leaving, only to return here to raise their children.

It was a simpler way of life. A community with strong values and people who knew and looked after their neighbors.

She, too, had left, convinced there was nothing here for her, but here she was. And, like Eve, McKenna figured the day would come when Faith would return and want the house, since she seemed to be the most attached to it.

"If you want your own house, you could build on the ranch," Eve suggested. "There's a nice spot to the east…." Her voice trailed off as if she realized she was wasting her breath. McKenna had already made up her mind.

"Did I hear you mention Harper House?" Faith asked as if finally coming full awake. "My friend who works for the county said it's going to be auctioned off."

"When?" McKenna asked.

"This Saturday, I think."

McKenna couldn't help her rush of excitement. This was obviously meant to be.

Faith laughed. "You *always* liked that place. I remember when you used to sneak over there even though Dad told us not to." She grinned. "I used to follow you."

"You used to ride over there?" Eve asked with a shake of her head. "Do you have any idea how dangerous that was?"

"We never believed that story about old wells on the place," Faith said. "I think Dad didn't want us around the people who lived there. They weren't friendly at all. But they sure had a lot of kids."

Eve shot a look at her youngest sister that McKenna recognized. It was Eve's can-you-really-be-that-naive? look.

"Harper House was a place for troubled boys," Eve said. "That's why Dad didn't want you riding over there. I can't believe you did it anyway," she said to McKenna. "Do you have any idea what could have happened to you?"

"Why didn't Dad just tell us that?" Faith asked, frowning.

"Because he knew the two of you," Eve said as she rose to take her plate to the sink. "You'd have gone over there just to see if the boys were really dangerous."

"Well," McKenna said with a sigh, "it's just an old, empty house now that Ellis Harper has died. But there's forty acres with a creek, trees, a barn and some outbuildings. It's exactly what I'm looking for and it's adjacent to our ranch land to the east."

Eve shook her head, worry in her gaze. "I think you're making a mistake, but I know how you are once you've made up your mind."

"I'm just like you," McKenna said with a grin.

Eve nodded. "That's what worries me."

Chapter Three

McKenna called her Realtor friend right after breakfast to find out what she knew about Harper House.

"You heard about the auction? Minimum bid is what is owed in back taxes, but I don't expect it to go much higher than that given the condition of the house. It's really a white elephant. Why don't you let me show you some houses that don't need so much work?"

"Don't try to talk me out of it," McKenna said with a laugh. It amazed her that April sold anything the way she always tried to discourage buyers. "If the price doesn't go too high, I intend to buy it."

She had worked all through college, saving the money her parents and Eve had sent her. She also had money from a savings account her grandma, Nina Mae Cross, had started for her when she was adopted into the family.

"With auctions, you just never know," April said. "But I can't imagine there would be that many people interested in the place. The property isn't bad, though. The fences are in pretty good shape, and it does border your family ranch, so that is definitely a plus. The barn needs a new roof. But you might want to just tear down the house and build something smaller on the land."

McKenna couldn't imagine doing that. Something about that house had always interested her. She had just hung up when her cell phone rang.

"Have I got *good* news for you," a female voice said.

She was about to hang up, thinking it was someone trying to sell her something, when she recognized the voice. *"Arlene?"*

"Who else?" Arlene Evans let out one of her braying laughs. She was a gangly, raw-boned ranch woman who'd had her share of problems over the last year or so, including her husband leaving her alone with two grown children still living at home and her oldest daughter in the state mental hospital.

McKenna had signed up for Arlene's rural online dating service at a weak moment—following a wedding and some champagne. She now regretted it greatly.

It wasn't a man she needed but the courage to do what she'd always wanted: start a horse ranch.

She'd loved paint horses from the first time she'd seen one. Descended from horses introduced by the Spanish conquistadors, paints were part of the herds of wild horses that once roamed these very plains.

With paints becoming popular with cowboys for cattle work, McKenna believed she could make a good living raising them. *If* she could get the Harper property for the right price at the auction Saturday. It was all she could think about.

"I've found you just the man," Arlene gushed. "He's perfect for you. I hear wedding bells already."

"Slow down," McKenna said, wishing she'd read the small print to see how she could get out of this.

"He's handsome, a hard worker, loves horses and long walks and…did I mention he's handsome?" Arlene laughed again, making McKenna wince. "He's going to be out of the cell phone service area until Saturday night, so he'll meet you at Northern Lights restaurant at seven. You're going to thank me for this."

McKenna groaned inwardly. There was no backing out at this late date, especially since calling him sounded like it was out of the question. But suddenly she was more than a little afraid to find out who Arlene Evans thought was her perfect man.

She only half listened to Arlene rattle on about the man as she thought of the auction and her plans for the future: a man was the last thing on her mind.

It wasn't until after she'd hung up that she realized she hadn't caught her date's name. Great. She thought about calling Arlene back but didn't want to put herself through another twenty minutes of hearing about how perfect this guy was for her.

In a town the size of Whitehorse, spotting the man should be easy enough at the restaurant Saturday evening.

McKenna quickly forgot about her date. The house would be open for viewing before the auction, but she couldn't wait. She had to take another look at the place, and this might be her only chance to spend a little time there alone.

ARLENE EVANS GLANCED away from her computer screen to see her daughter Charlotte sprawled on the couch.

Just moments before that Arlene had been feeling pretty good. Her Internet rural dating service had taken off. Several of the matches she'd made had led to the altar. She'd always known she had a knack for this, even if she'd failed miserably with her own children.

For years she'd tried to find someone for her

oldest daughter, Violet—with no luck at all. A lot of that was Violet's doing, she had to admit now. Violet was crazy—and dangerous—so no wonder no man had wanted to take that on.

Now Violet was locked up in a mental institution—hopefully never to be released, if Arlene had anything to do with it.

Bo, Arlene's only son, had been engaged to Maddie Cavanaugh. The two had been all wrong for each other from the beginning. Unfortunately, since the breakup, though, Bo hadn't shown any interest in finding himself a good woman to spend the rest of his life with. In fact, when Arlene had offered to line him up with one of her clients, he'd told her it would be over his dead body. It broke her heart, since Bo had always been her favorite.

And then there was Charlotte, the daughter that Arlene had thought would never have any trouble finding a husband.

Arlene scowled as she studied her youngest child—and Charlotte's huge protruding belly. For months Arlene had been trying to find out who had fathered the baby now growing inside her daughter. The baby was due next month, and Arlene was no closer to discovering the name of the father than she'd been when she'd found out about the pregnancy.

Charlotte took perverse pleasure in keeping it

a secret. *If* her daughter even knew, Arlene thought with a silent curse. Other mothers considered their children blessings. Arlene had come to see hers as a curse.

Not for the first time, Arlene saw a silver SUV drive past. She couldn't see the driver, not with the glint of the June sun on the darkened side window, but she had the impression it was a woman behind the wheel.

Arlene frowned, trying to remember how many other times she'd seen the vehicle. Strange, since not much traffic ever came down this road. She put it out of her mind. She had a lot more important things to worry about.

When she turned back to her computer, she was surprised to see that she had a potential new client. She completely forgot about the silver SUV as she clicked on the man's e-mail and felt a small thrill that had nothing to do with success or money.

Since my wife died, I find myself deeply needing the company of an interesting woman. I want someone who would like to travel the world with me. Someone who wants to share my final years.

Travel the world. What woman wouldn't want to do that with an attractive older man? A man only a little older than Arlene herself.

She e-mailed Hank Monroe back, promising to find him the perfect woman and set up a time to meet.

BEHIND HARPER HOUSE, Nate Dempsey leaned on his shovel to rest for a moment and listened to the sound of the wind in the trees. A hot, dry wind that made his skin ache. The years must have distorted his memory. He'd been so sure he was digging in the right place.

But the land looked different than he remembered, and it had been a long time ago.

He began to dig again, turning over one shovelful of dirt after another, trying to gauge how deep the body would have been buried.

As he dug, he tried not to think about that hot summer night. Not the sounds he'd heard. Nor the fear he'd felt knowing he could be next. What he hadn't known was who they were burying out back. He didn't know that until the next morning. Until it was too late.

The heat bore down on him. He stopped digging for a moment to look up at the blue wind-scoured sky overhead and catch his breath. Standing there, it was impossible not to think of the past. Had a day gone by that he hadn't remembered this place?

He'd spent years looking over his shoulder, knowing whose face he would see that instant before he felt the blade. But now he was no longer that skinny, scared boy. Nor was he a man willing to run from his past any longer. It would end here.

He began to dig again. Had it really been twenty-one years since he'd left this godforsaken place? Coming back here, it felt as if it had only been yesterday.

His shovel hit something that made the blade ring. He shuddered at the sound as he looked down, expecting to see bones. Just a rock. No body buried here.

He stopped again, this time the skin on the back of his neck prickling. As he had earlier, he felt someone was watching him. Carrying the shovel with him, he strode back to the house and stripped off his shirt to use it to wipe the sweat from his eyes.

For a moment he stood at the back door, surveying the land behind the house, the tall, old cottonwoods that followed the creek bed, the weather-beaten barn and outbuildings, the rolling grassy hillsides.

He couldn't see anyone, but that didn't mean Roy Vaughn wasn't there. He was the man Nate had to fear now, just as he had as a boy.

Stepping inside, he turned on the faucet at the old kitchen sink, letting the water run until it came up icy-cold, all the time watching out the window. He could almost convince himself he'd only imagined that someone was watching him.

Discarding his shirt, he scooped up handfuls of water, drinking them down greedily. Johnny's remains were out there somewhere. With all his heart he wished it wasn't true. That Johnny had run away, just as he'd been told. But he knew better. Johnny would have come back for him if he'd gotten away. Johnny wouldn't have left him at Harper House. Not when Johnny had known how dangerous the place was for Nate.

As he turned off the faucet and wiped his wet hands on his jeans, he gazed out the back window again.

Ellis Harper hadn't let anyone near the house in years. That meant no one else would have had a chance to dig up the body and hide it, right? He'd come as soon as he'd learned of Harper's death. But had he come too late?

Bare-chested, he went back out and began to dig again in a different spot, the heat growing more intense. He dug down deep enough, turning over a final shovelful of dirt, and looked down into the hole seeing nothing but more earth.

This was the area where he'd thought they'd buried the body. He'd stake his life on it. Hell, he *was* staking his life on it.

There was just one problem.

The body was gone. If it had ever been here.

CRICKETS CHIRPED IN the tall grass as McKenna dismounted, loosely tied her horse and slipped between the logs of the jack fence.

The grass brushed her jeans, making a swishing sound as she moved through it toward the house. She listened for the sound of a rattlesnake, telling herself not only was she trespassing but her father could have been right about the dangers—including snakes.

A stiff breeze at the edge of the house banged a loose shutter and whipped her hair into her face. She stopped to look around for a moment, feeling as if she was being watched. But there was no vehicle parked in the drive. No sign that anyone had been here in a very long time.

She tried the screen door on the front porch first. The door groaned open. The wind caught it, jerked the handle from her fingers and slammed the door against the wall.

McKenna thought she heard an accompanying thud from inside the house, as if someone had bumped into something. She froze, imagining Ellis Harper coming out with a shotgun. But Ellis was dead. And she didn't believe in ghosts, right? *"Hello?"*

No answer.

"Hello?" she called a little louder.

Another thud, this one deeper in the house. She stepped to the front door, knocked and, receiving no answer, cupped her hands to peer through the window next to the door.

The house was empty except for dust. That's why the recent footprints caught her attention. The tracks were male-size boot soles. Someone from the county would have been out to check the house before the auction, she told herself.

The tracks led into the kitchen at the back. What she saw leaning by the back door made her reconsider going inside. A shovel, fresh dirt caked on it, stood against the wall. Next to it was a plaid shirt where someone had dropped it on the floor.

Her horse whinnied over at the fence. Another horse whinnied back, the sound coming from behind the house.

Someone was here.

Not someone from the county, who would have driven out and parked in front. Someone who'd come by horseback. Someone who didn't want to be seen? Just like her?

Ellis Harper's funeral had been earlier this week. Anyone who read the paper would know the house was empty.

But why would that person be digging?

She retreated as quietly as possible across the porch and down the steps. As she angled back toward where she'd left her horse, she glanced behind the house.

There appeared to be several areas on the

hillside where the earth had been freshly turned. She hadn't noticed it earlier; all her attention had been on the house. As she reached the fence and quickly slipped through, her horse whinnied again. The mare's whinny was answered, drawing McKenna's gaze to the hillside beyond the barn in time to see a rider on a gray Appaloosa horse.

From this distance she could see that the rider was a man. He was shirtless, no doubt because he'd left his plaid shirt in the house where he'd discarded it along with the shovel.

She caught only a glimpse of him, his head covered by a Western straw hat, as he topped the hill and disappeared as if in a hurry to get away.

She wondered who he was. Obviously someone who wasn't supposed to be here—just like herself. She hadn't gotten a good enough look at him and knew she wouldn't be able to recognize him if she saw him again, but she would his horse. It was a spotted Appaloosa, the ugliest coloring she'd ever seen—and that was saying a lot.

As she swung up into her saddle, she couldn't help but wonder what the man had been digging for—and if he'd found it.

ARLENE CALLED HANK Monroe to confirm their appointment to sign him up for her rural dating service before she headed into Whitehorse. The first thing that had struck her was his voice. It was deep and soft and sent a small thrill through her. Had any man's voice ever done that before? Not that she could remember—but then, she was no spring chicken anymore.

She knew she was setting herself up for disappointment. The man couldn't be as good as he sounded either in his e-mail or on the phone.

"I'm looking forward to meeting you," he'd said. "I have to confess, I've never done anything like this before. You know, dating online. The way my generation did it was gazes across a crowded room. I'm a little nervous."

She'd assured him there was nothing to it.

But Arlene was nervous herself when she reached the Hi-Line Café where they'd agreed to meet.

The moment she walked in and spotted Hank Monroe sitting at one of the booths her heart began to pound wildly. Never in her life had she experienced such a reaction.

She'd been pregnant with Violet when she married Floyd Evans. It had been the result of a one-night stand. She'd said she was on the Pill so he wouldn't take her right home. Floyd had been good-looking and popular, and she'd thought she could fall in love with him—and him with her if he'd give her a chance.

She'd also erroneously thought that she wouldn't get pregnant.

She'd been wrong on all counts.

But when she'd discovered she was pregnant, Floyd had seemed as good a bet as anyone. He had a farm down in Old Town Whitehorse and, while reluctant, he had agreed at the urging of his parents to stand up and accept his responsibilities.

She'd known she was no looker. It was one reason she'd learned to cook at an early age. She'd realized she needed more to offer than other girls. She'd thought her cooking and cleaning would make Floyd fall in love with her. She'd still dreamed of the happily-ever-after romance she hadn't found with Floyd or any other boy.

She'd been only seventeen when she and Floyd had married. He'd been twenty-eight. Now, at fifty-one, Arlene had long ago given up on love, let alone romance.

Hank Monroe looked up just then. He wasn't handsome, not by anyone's standards, but there was something about him that had her pulse pounding as she made her way to his booth.

"Arlene?" he asked hopefully as he got to his big feet.

She could only nod and smile. "You must be Hank."

He nodded with a laugh that resembled a donkey's bray. She laughed then, too, and they exchanged a look that made Arlene feel seventeen again.

"I like your laugh," he said and grinned.

By the time she had him signed up for her dating service she had a date with him for Saturday night and was on her way to buy herself something special to wear.

She couldn't remember the last time she'd been this excited. But at the back of her mind she heard her mother's nagging voice warning her that this feeling wouldn't last. It couldn't. Because Arlene didn't deserve to be happy.

HAD VIOLET EVANS known what her mother was feeling at that moment, she would have joined her deceased grandmother in warning Arlene not to count on a future—let alone a happy one.

If Violet had her way, her mother wouldn't be around long. And from what the doctors were saying at the mental hospital, it looked as if Violet was going to get her way.

And not even Arlene—who'd seen through Violet's ruse—could stop her. In fact, Arlene Evans might be the only person alive who knew how sick—and dangerous—her daughter really was.

But while Violet hadn't fooled her mother, she

had her doctors. As Violet sat next to the window and looked over the hospital grounds, she could almost taste freedom. It wouldn't be long now. She'd played her role perfectly. All those case histories of psychosis had given her the script. Now she was nearing the final act, the one that would get her released.

It didn't surprise her that her mother was fighting her release. Arlene knew what Violet was capable of and, worse, had an inkling of what she *would* do once she got out of this place. Violet's great sin, she believed, was that she'd shamed her mother by not being marriageable.

She'd been born unattractive and hadn't grown out of it. Even her mother—who Violet resembled—had snagged a man. Arlene's endless attempts at marrying her off had only made matters worse. Violet hated her for it. Hated that she'd taken after her mother, unlike her two siblings.

"Violet? Is everything all right?"

She turned to find her doctor watching her closely, a slight frown on his face.

"I was just thinking about some of the awful things my mother said I did," she covered quickly as she realized he'd seen her true feelings when he'd walked up on her.

She really had to be more careful.

He sat down beside her. He was a small man with small hands. "Does that make you angry?"

"Only with myself," she said piously. She'd worked so hard to hide what was really going on inside her. She would have to remember not to think about her mother.

"I am getting better, aren't I, Dr. Armond?" she asked pleadingly.

"Yes, Violet. I am very pleased with your prognosis. Very pleased. In fact, that was one reason I came to find you." He paused and smiled. "I'm recommending your release."

Violet's heart leaped. "Oh, Dr. Armond. Are you sure I'm ready?"

"Yes, Violet. I'll recommend some outpatient visits, of course, but there is no reason you can't be an active member of society again. I'd hoped you would be excited."

"Oh, I am. I can't wait. To think that I have my whole life ahead of me…" Her eyes brimmed with tears and he covered her hand with his.

"I'm so glad to hear that because I've set your release for next month."

Next month? She'd been planning on getting out sooner than that. What was wrong with the stupid old quack?

She was careful not to let her disappointment or her anger show. She tried to calm herself. What was another thirty days here? Nothing compared to what she'd been through. But it still felt like a lifetime, she was so anxious to get out.

"I wanted you to have enough time to prepare for reentering that world," he was saying. "I think it would be unhealthy for you to return to your mother's home given the way she feels, don't you?"

"Yes."

"I thought you could prepare by working here in the hospital office. You'll also need income. I'll help you put together a résumé for when you're released."

The imbecile. She wasn't going to need a job when she got out. "That is so kind of you," she said. "How can I ever thank you?" She could think of several ways she'd like to thank him, all of them involving his pain.

"You being well and getting on with your life will be thanks enough," he said as he removed his hand from hers and rose to leave. "I want you to be a survivor, Violet."

She nodded and smiled. "I intend to be." She couldn't say the same for her mother and the others who had made her life a living hell.

She tried not to shudder at the thought of the mediocre life she would have on the outside if it was up to these doctors. Some dismal job, a cramped apartment, several cats and nothing to look forward to at night but television and a frozen cheesecake.

A woman as smart as she was? Not a chance.

She'd been foolish in the past. She'd let them catch her. She wouldn't make that mistake again..

She thought about her mother's face when she saw her oldest daughter again. Payback was a bitch, she thought with a secret smile as she looked out the window.

Thirty days. And counting.

Chapter Four

The auction was held in front of the Harper House on a bright blue-sky June day. Someone had mowed part of the weeds in the front yard the night before. The air smelled of fresh-mown grass and dust from the county road out front.

As McKenna mounted the steps to the open front door, she saw that the footprints she'd seen yesterday evening in the thick layer of dust had been trampled by the half dozen people who'd traipsed through the house this morning.

April had been right. The house needed work. But that wasn't what surprised McKenna. She'd always been enthralled by the house. She'd just assumed she would feel the same once inside. The interior had a dark, cold feel even with the warm sun shining through the dirty windows, and she found herself shivering as she walked through the rooms.

She noticed the shovel and shirt she'd seen by

the back door yesterday were gone. On the third floor, when she looked out a small back window, she couldn't see the places where the man had dug. They'd apparently been covered with cut weeds. Had she not caught the man in the act yesterday, she would never have guessed anyone had been digging on the hillside.

It still made her wonder what he might have been looking for, but she turned her attention to the house as she wandered from room to room, trying to imagine herself living here. It was hard given the condition of the house. It would take days just to clean, let alone paint. She knew exactly what her sister Eve would say.

Raze the house and start over.

McKenna had heard several such comments from the other people who had gathered for the auction.

"There's a nice building spot upon the hill once the house is gone," she'd heard one man say.

But the rooms were spacious, and she told herself once the house was cleaned up, painted and furnished she could be happy here. Anyway, the house was the reason she'd always wanted the place, wasn't it?

At one fifty-five she gathered with the others in the front yard as the auctioneer climbed the porch steps and cleared his throat to quiet the small crowd.

McKenna glanced at the group around her, surprised that some of the people who'd toured the house earlier had left. Just curiosity seekers. She recognized only one elderly man and his wife, Edgar and Ethel Winthrop. The couple lived about two miles to the north. McKenna was surprised they'd stayed, since she doubted they would be bidding on the place.

She didn't recognize any of the others waiting. Three of the men appeared to be in their early thirties; the fourth man, in his forties, was on a cell phone. She figured he was here bidding for an investor and turned her attention to the other three men.

One, clearly a local rancher, wore a Mint Bar cap, a worn canvas coat and work boots and had a toothpick sticking out the side of his mouth. The second was dressed in a dinosaur T-shirt, jeans and athletic shoes. The third man wore jeans, cowboy boots, a Western shirt and a gray Stetson.

As the auctioneer described the property and the county auction requirements, she saw another man, one she hadn't noticed before. He'd parked on the county road some distance from the proceedings and now stood, his arms crossed over his chest as he leaned against the front of his pickup truck, his battered Western straw hat pulled low against the sun.

He'd obviously just come to watch. He was dressed in work boots, jeans and a white T-shirt that called attention to his tanned, muscular arms. There was a toolbox in the back of his truck and a construction logo of some kind on the cab, but she couldn't make out the name from where she stood.

"If everyone's ready, let's begin," the auctioneer said, drawing her attention back to the front.

The cowboy glanced over at her as the auctioneer began the bidding. He was good-looking enough to make her do a double take.

"I can't believe anyone would buy that house," Ethel Winthrop whispered behind McKenna.

"Not everyone cares about a house's history, Ethel," her husband whispered back.

"Who would like to start the bidding?" the auctioneer inquired.

When no one responded, the auctioneer started the bid high and had to drop the price when there were no takers.

McKenna waited as the man on the cell phone bid along with dinosaur-shirt man and the local rancher. The cowboy hadn't bid either, she noticed, apparently waiting as she was. Or maybe he'd just come to watch.

As the price rose, the man on the cell phone quit bidding and left. It had come down between the rancher and dino-shirt man when the cowboy jumped in. McKenna feared the men were going to drive the price up too high for her.

The rancher quit. It was down to the cowboy and the dino-shirt man when McKenna finally bid.

The cowboy shot her a look and raised her bid.

She bid two more times, dino-shirt dropping out, so it was just her and the cowboy. One look into his dark eyes and she realized he was enjoying himself—at her expense.

"The young woman has the bid," the auctioneer said after they'd gone back and forth.

Time seemed to stop, and then the cowboy tipped his hat, his dark eyes flashing. "It's the lady's."

McKenna couldn't believe it.

The auctioneer closed the bidding. Edgar Winthrop stepped up to congratulate her and ask her what she planned to do with the house as the remainder of the small group dispersed.

"I'm going to live here," she said and saw his wife's expression.

"Not alone, I hope," she said.

"Ethel," the husband said in a warning tone.

"Edgar, she should know about that house," the elderly woman insisted. "If she moves in and then finds out…"

The husband took his wife's arm. "You'll have to excuse my wife. All houses have a history,

Ethel." He smiled at McKenna. "I wouldn't concern yourself with local gossip. What's past is past, right?"

McKenna smiled, too excited to care about the house's history. Anyway, she figured the woman was referring to the troubled boys who'd lived on the place when she was a girl. They couldn't have been any worse than she and her sisters.

"Congratulations, I'm sure it will make you a fine home," Edgar said.

"I'm sure it will, too," she agreed.

He tugged at his wife's elbow, but Ethel grabbed McKenna's sleeve. "If you need us, we live up that way as the crow flies." She pointed north.

"Thank you," McKenna said as Edgar Winthrop took his wife's hand and led her toward their car.

"You remember what I said," Ethel called over her shoulder.

"I will, thank you." She turned, looking for the cowboy who'd given up the bid to her, but he'd apparently left right away.

As she moved up to the porch to take care of the paperwork, she noticed the man who'd parked on the road and watched from a distance also leaving. While she couldn't see his face in the shadow of his Western straw hat, she had the impression he was upset.

IF NATE DEMPSEY HAD been superstitious, he would have gotten the hell out of Whitehorse the moment he'd seen the blond cowgirl again.

When he'd seen her in the small crowd that had gathered for the auction, he'd hoped she was here out of curiosity and nothing more. Ultimately he'd hoped that no one would bid on Harper House or that the minimum bid would be too high and that the house would remain empty just long enough for him to finish what he'd come here to do.

But that hope had been shot to hell the moment the young blonde began to bid. He'd seen her interest in the house when she'd come around the place before.

When she kept bidding, he knew she was determined to have Harper House.

When the dust settled, the bidding done, the blonde had the house. McKenna Bailey. He'd discovered he'd been right about her living nearby. Her family owned the ranch adjacent to the property. The Bailey girls, as they were known in these parts, had a reputation for being rough-and-tumble cowgirls with a streak of independence that ran as deep as their mule-headedness.

McKenna Bailey had proven that today.

Not the kind of woman who would be easily intimidated.

But as he drove away from Harper House he

knew he had to find a way to make sure McKenna Bailey didn't get in his way. He'd waited so long to end this, and now she had unknowingly put herself in the middle of more trouble than she could imagine.

He cursed the way his luck was going as he raced north toward the small Western town, ruing the day he'd ever laid eyes on Whitehorse, Montana—and McKenna Bailey.

BY THAT EVENING McKenna was actually in the mood for a date—even a blind one—as she walked into Northern Lights restaurant. She was still floating on air from the excitement of her purchase earlier that afternoon, although she hadn't had much time to look the place over after signing all the papers.

She couldn't wait to take her horse out and ride her property.

Northern Lights restaurant had been opened just before Christmas by McKenna's friend Laci Cavanaugh and her fiancé Bridger Duvall. It was *the* place to eat in Whitehorse. The fact that her date had chosen it gave McKenna hope.

She was instantly disappointed, though, when she was told by a young waitress she didn't know that Laci wasn't working tonight and that Bridger was swamped back in the kitchen.

"Are you dining alone?" the waitress asked.

She certainly hoped not. As she glanced around the restaurant, she spotted a lone male sitting off in one corner. He raised his head and got to his feet when he saw her.

He was the good-looking cowboy who'd bid against her at the auction earlier that day. Just her luck. And his.

"Small world, huh?" he said with an ironic smile.

This was her *date?* She remembered the way he'd tipped his hat to her when he quit bidding. She was pretty sure that had been anger she'd seen in his dark eyes.

"You look like you could use a drink. I know I could." He motioned to the waitress before turning back to McKenna. "What'll you have? Hell, you probably want champagne to celebrate, don't you? Give us a bottle of your best."

The waitress took off before McKenna could stop her. The last thing she wanted to do was have dinner with this man, let alone celebrate with him.

He held out his hand. "Flynn Garrett."

His hand swallowed hers. "McKenna—"

"Bailey," he finished for her. "Yeah, I know." His smile broadened as he seemed to take her in. "The woman who bought herself a house and forty acres today. No hard feelings. You won fair and square. So let's celebrate."

He pulled out a chair for her and waited.

She tried to think of a good reason to break the date, but then the champagne arrived and she found herself taking a seat as the cork was popped and Flynn made a show of pouring them each a glass.

"To you, Miss Bailey," he said, tapping his glass against hers.

His dark eyes never left hers as he took a sip. "Hmm, not bad," he said, although she was almost positive he would have rather had another beer like the one he'd been nursing when she'd arrived.

She tried to relax. Blind dates were nerve-racking enough without her ending up having dinner with the man she'd outbid. A very handsome man, she might add.

"You're a tough woman to beat at her own game," he said, his gaze hard to read. She'd put her money on him still being angry. She'd bet he was the kind of man who didn't like to lose.

"If it makes you feel any better, you drove the bid up so high I have very little money left for improvements."

He appeared shocked. "You aren't considering doing anything with that house?"

"Yes. Why?" She watched the way he nervously took a drink of his champagne. "What had *you* planned to do with it?"

"Burn it down."

Now it was her turn to be shocked. "You aren't serious."

"I just wanted the land. The house is in such bad shape…" He frowned. "Sorry, I'm sure you don't want to hear that."

"It needs work, I'll admit, but structurally—"

"You planning to do the work yourself?"

She bristled. "I'll have you know I'm capable of doing just about anything I set my mind to."

He nodded slowly, eyeing her with an intensity that made her a little nervous. "I bet you are."

The waitress brought the menus and he disappeared behind his. McKenna told herself that he was still angry with her for outbidding her and that he wouldn't have bid so high if he hadn't wanted the house as well as the land. What he said about the condition of the house was just sour grapes.

"How are the steaks here?" he asked over the top of his menu. His eyes were almost black. "You look like a woman who could handle a steak." He put down his menu as the waitress appeared and grinned at McKenna. "Am I wrong?"

She ordered a rib eye, rare, which made him chuckle. He ordered the largest T-bone the restaurant served, also rare.

"So tell me about McKenna Bailey," he said,

leaning forward to rest his forearms on the table, those dark eyes intent on her again.

"And bore you to tears?"

He shook his head. "There is nothing boring about you, and we both know it. Why White-horse? Come on, I really want to know."

"I was born and raised here."

His eyebrow shot up. "No kidding."

"Well, that's somewhat true," she amended with a smile. "I was adopted when I was born. My adopted family lives in Old Town White-horse. That's where I grew up."

"You're adopted?" That seemed to interest him.

"I didn't find out until recently."

"No one told you?"

She shook her head. "If you knew my adoptive mother, that would make sense to you. She said the moment she laid eyes on my sisters and me we were hers and nobody else's, and that's why she didn't tell us. Lila Bailey Jackson is a very strong, determined woman."

"Like her daughter." He took a sip of his champagne, then frowned. "Lila Bailey *Jackson?*"

"She recently married Loren Jackson. It's a long story, but apparently they were in love for years."

"Jackson," he repeated softly. "Like the sheriff?" He refilled her glass. She hadn't realized she'd emptied it already. Nerves.

"The sheriff is Loren's son and my sister Eve's fiancé. It's a small town," she added with a laugh and realized she was starting to enjoy herself. And why shouldn't she? She did have something to celebrate, and her date was just as handsome as Arlene had said.

She hadn't dated all that much, too busy between school and a job working for a local veterinarian in Bozeman while she'd attended Montana State University. It felt good to be in the company of an attractive cowboy.

"So tell me about you."

He shrugged. "Not much to tell. Raised on a ranch, like you."

Had she told him she was raised on a ranch? She couldn't remember.

"I've worked all over, wrangling and doing odd jobs. Once you turn thirty you can't help but think about planting roots. Not too deep, though," he quickly amended. "I like being a free spirit. When I leave here I'm thinking of going to South America. Like Butch Cassidy and the Sundance Kid. You know, they robbed a train up here right before they went to South America."

Allegedly. But she didn't tell him that. She knew Flynn Garrett's type. He liked to think of himself as an outlaw. He'd used his looks to get him through life, always taking the path of least resistance. She'd dated a few boys like him in college. They were fun. At least for a while.

"So why did you bid on the old Harper place?" she asked and took a drink of her champagne. She might as well celebrate because she'd just bought herself a house and forty acres.

He shrugged in answer. "I like competition."

She eyed him over the rim of her champagne glass. Yeah? But he wasn't as good at losing as he was at pretending, she thought. The question was: had he wanted Harper House or did he just not want anyone else to have it?

"What will you do now?" she asked.

"I don't know. You've forced me to change my plans." He smiled at her as if he thought he could con her into thinking she owed him. Not likely.

"Sorry," she said with a grin, "but I've always wanted that place."

"Really? Why?"

She shook her head. "I wish I knew."

Flynn seemed lost in thought for a long moment, and she wondered if he understood the pull of Harper House more than he was admitting.

She felt a kinship with him because of the house. It was odd. She'd just met him earlier today and yet it was as if she'd known him a lot longer. Which made this date a little sad, since she didn't think she would be going out with him again.

Flynn poured them both more champagne, emptying the bottle. "Don't worry about me," he said as if there hadn't been a lag in the conversation. "I'm a man who always lands on his feet, one way or another. Meanwhile, I'm having dinner with a beautiful, fascinating woman." His expression was so intense she was glad that the waitress appeared with their salads.

The conversation turned to horses during dinner and that awkward moment passed. McKenna realized that he'd either guessed about her love of horses or someone had told him. But then, that would mean that he'd asked around about her. Arlene. How had McKenna forgotten that Arlene had set this up?

She recalled how Arlene had been so confident this man would be perfect for her. She really should cancel her membership in Arlene's dating service first thing in the morning. If only she'd read the contract more closely.

The evening passed quickly, and suddenly they were at that uncomfortable end of the date where he walked her out to her pickup and she feared he would kiss her.

And feared he wouldn't.

His kiss was nice. Soft, sweet, tentative. What surprised her was that she sensed a vulnerability in him when he kissed her that he'd kept well hidden in the time she'd been around him. Flynn

Garrett didn't have it all together as much as he wanted everyone to believe.

He drew back from the kiss, and she was surprised to see regret in his gaze. As he turned and walked away, she could only assume she wouldn't be seeing him again.

Chapter Five

The ringing of her cell phone wrenched McKenna out of a terrifying dream in which she was running for her life.

She jerked up in the bed, her heart pounding, her nightshirt stuck to her skin with sweat.

"Hello?"

"McKenna, I wanted to catch you before you took off this morning."

She glanced at the clock. It wasn't even six o'clock. *"Arlene?"* If she was calling to see how McKenna's date had gone—

"I didn't want you to feel bad about what happened last night. These things happen, although I *was* surprised. He seemed like such a nice young man. And he was so interested in you I couldn't imagine why he'd cancel."

"What?" She was still caught in the dream; danger hunkered in the room like dense fog, making everything seem surreal.

"I just feel bad because I couldn't get hold of you to tell you. I tried your cell. You must have had it turned off. And when I called the restaurant to give you a heads-up—"

"Arlene, what are you talking about?"

"Your date last night. I just hate that he stood you up, but I have someone else who I think—"

"Wait a minute." McKenna sat up straighter and rubbed her free hand over her face as she tried to make sense of what Arlene was saying. "I wasn't stood up."

"You mean he changed his mind and met you at the restaurant after all?" Arlene let out a relieved laugh. "Good, I wasn't wrong about him. I told you Nate Dempsey was perfect for you. I'm so glad he showed up. I do wish he'd let me know, though. If he'd read the dating service agreement, he'd have—"

"Nate Dempsey?" McKenna repeated.

"Your *date.*" Arlene laughed. "It must have been some night if you don't remember his name."

Arlene was mixed up. McKenna regretted the day she'd signed up for the online dating service.

"Arlene, my date was with *Flynn Garrett.* Not anyone named Nate Dempsey."

Silence. An anomaly for Arlene.

McKenna felt her first sense of unease. "My date *was* with Flynn, right?"

"I've never heard of a Flynn Garrett," Arlene said at last. "*Who* did you have dinner with last night?" she asked, sounding horrified.

It was too early in the morning for this. "Arlene, I have to go." McKenna hung up and replayed the scene at the restaurant. She'd just assumed that Flynn was her date. Now that she thought about it, he'd never mentioned the online dating service—and neither had she.

She felt a little foolish. But, then again, no harm had been done. She'd enjoyed dinner and Flynn Garrett.

Unfortunately, she couldn't help but wonder who this Nate Dempsey was. And why he'd canceled his date with her at the last minute. Arlene said he'd been "so interested" in her?

Not that it mattered, she thought as she gave up on returning to sleep and headed for the shower in an attempt to throw off the remnants of the nightmare she'd been having before Arlene's phone call. Her legs felt weak as if she really had been running for her life. The dream emerged again. She had a flash of Harper House. It had been dark in the dream. She'd been running away from the house, she thought with a chill, because someone had been chasing her.

Turning on the shower, she climbed under the spray, determined to forget the nightmare. She had a big day ahead of her. Once she had the house cleaned she could start painting. She was anxious to get her horses on the property and get moved in.

Her sister Faith was still asleep, and Eve was over at her own house this morning as McKenna left. She drove through Old Town Whitehorse—what was left of it, which was only a few buildings.

Old Town was the first settlement of Whitehorse. It had been nearer the Missouri River, in the country McKenna had grown up in. But when the railroad came through in the 1800s, most of the town migrated five miles north, taking the name with it.

The original settlement of Whitehorse was now little more than a ghost town except for a handful of buildings, including the community center and the one-room school-house, in the area now referred to as Old Town.

The Baileys had been one of the first families, along with the Cavanaughs and the Jacksons, to settle in the original Whitehorse. That was one reason McKenna had wanted to buy closer to her family's ranch. This was where her history was. By buying the Harper property she would be continuing a tradition around Old Town.

She was thinking about that—and the roots she would be putting down—when she parked her truck across the street from the hardware store.

As she got out of her pickup, she heard the train pull in.

The tracks were just across a small town park. Today it was the Amtrak passenger train coming through, the only line in the state that provided service as far west as Seattle or east to Chicago.

As the train slowed to a stop to pick up several waiting passengers, McKenna heard a horse whinny and turned to see a truck and horse trailer a few vehicles ahead of hers. Nothing unusual about seeing horses in trailers on the main street in this part of Montana.

What caught her eye was the horse sticking his head out the side of the trailer. It was a spotted Appaloosa, and even before she walked over to get a closer look she knew she'd seen this horse before—and where.

"I wouldn't do that if I were you," said a deep male voice behind her. "Old Blue is pretty temperamental."

She pulled her hand back from the horse's neck and turned. From behind her, the Appaloosa nuzzled her shoulder and snuffled her hair.

"That's odd—he usually doesn't take to strangers," the man said with a shake of his head and a wry smile. He rested his hands on his jean-clad hips and eyed her from under the brim of his straw hat.

"I have a way with horses," she said after her initial shock had passed at recognizing him as well as the horse.

"I can see that." He was the man she'd seen parked on the road at the auction, the one who'd been standing back, leaning against his pickup, watching from a distance.

She'd taken him for a construction worker when she'd seen him at the auction because of the logo on his truck, she recalled. The night before that, when she'd seen him ride over the hill behind Harper House on this Appaloosa, she'd taken him for a trespasser like herself.

Now she was more than a little curious about his interest in her house and why he'd been digging the evening before the auction on what was now her property.

"The first time I saw this horse I knew I would recognize him if I ever saw him again." She chuckled. "Imagine my surprise at seeing him again. And *you*."

"I guess it's a small world," he said, smiling back at her.

"Not *that* small." She glanced at the Montana license plate on the back of his pickup. Park County. He was a long way from home. Taking a step back, she craned her neck to see the logo on the side of his truck.

Dempsey Construction.

No wonder she'd thought he worked construction.

Dempsey?

Her gaze shot back to the man. "*Nate* Dempsey?" She couldn't believe this. *This* was the man Arlene thought would be perfect for her?

He wasn't nearly as good-looking as Flynn Garrett, although he was nicely built, tall with slim hips and muscular broad shoulders. His eyes were a warm, rich brown, and his hair that curled at the nape of his neck under his Western straw hat was a darker blond than her own.

Lantern-jawed, his features were rugged and rough, like a man who'd been in his share of fist-fights. But when he smiled, well, there was something about him that made her heart beat a little faster.

"I'm McKenna Bailey," she said. "The woman you stood up last night."

At least he had the good grace to look sheepish. "I can explain about that."

She cocked her head and crossed her arms over her chest. "This ought to be good."

NATE CURSED HIMSELF for making the date. At the time he'd thought it necessary to find out how much of a threat McKenna Bailey might be, and Arlene Evans had been a wealth of information about McKenna and the Baileys.

But after he'd seen McKenna at the auction yesterday the date hadn't been necessary. In fact, he'd felt the date would be dangerous. He hadn't wanted her to know who he was. Let alone what he was doing in Whitehorse.

Now, though, he saw that standing her up had been a mistake.

McKenna Bailey was everything he'd heard she was—and more. She was trouble in a pair of slim-fitting jeans and boots. And if he wasn't careful, she would get him killed.

"I didn't stand you up," he said. "Not exactly," he added quickly. "I called Arlene and told her I couldn't make it because I was running so late, then I realized after I hung up that you would already be at the restaurant. So I dropped everything and hurried into town, but then I saw you having dinner with some other man...." He shrugged, amazed how easily lying came back to him.

"I thought he *was* my date," she said, looking a little less angry.

"I can see where you could mix us up, especially if his name was Nate Dempsey, too."

She flushed. "I forgot to get a name from Arlene when she told me about the date. I just assumed since this other man was at the restaurant alone..." She groaned, realizing she was digging herself in deeper.

He smiled at her, letting her off the hook even though he enjoyed seeing her flustered. He doubted that happened often. "I'm the one who's sorry. Apparently we just weren't meant to have dinner last night."

"Apparently," she said and glanced toward his horse trailer and old Blue, his horse. "So now you're leaving town?"

"What gave you that idea?" he asked.

"Your license plates." She narrowed those oh-so-blue eyes of hers at him. "You're not from around here, but you look familiar."

"I just have that kind of face," he said, feeling the heat of her gaze.

She was still eyeing him. "So what brings you to Whitehorse?"

He smiled. "You sound like a cop."

"Have you been interrogated by a lot of cops?"

He laughed, shaking his head at her. "I thought I explained about dinner."

"You did," she said, nodding in agreement. "Now I'm just wondering what you were digging for the other evening out at the old Harper place."

So she *had* seen him riding away. *"Digging?"*

Her hands went to her hips, her eyes narrowed again. "Shovel. Dirt. Red-and-blue-plaid shirt. Appaloosa horse. That horse," she said, turning to point at Blue.

"I admit I was out there riding the property, but

I'm afraid I didn't do any digging," he said. What was one more lie?

She frowned, seeming not so sure now. "Well, *someone* was there digging. I wonder who it was?"

He shrugged. "When I rode the perimeter of the property I noticed that the fences are in good shape. Better shape than I thought they'd be in."

"If you were interested in the property, then why didn't you bid?"

"I was just looking for a cheap place to board my horse while I'm in town. Truthfully, I really didn't think anyone would bid on the house and I thought…" He smiled. He did have a great smile.

"You thought you could leave your horse out there for free," she finished for him.

"Not just my horse. I saw a spot on that creek in the cottonwoods that would have been perfect to pitch my tent."

She glanced at his rig and he could almost read her mind. Neither the truck nor the horse trailer came cheap. "You don't look exactly destitute."

He shook his head. "I have some business in town, but I'm trying to make it feel more like a vacation. I've always preferred the outdoors and like to camp." He shrugged.

"I'm sorry I ruined your plans," McKenna said, thinking how she'd also messed up Flynn Garrett's plans. She, apparently, was just that kind of woman.

"So what are you planning to do with the place?" Nate Dempsey asked.

"Live there."

"You aren't serious."

She bristled.

"Sorry. I saw the state the house is in. I'm sure it would be cheaper to start fresh with a new house."

She really was getting tired of hearing this. "It's going to take a lot of work, but I'm not afraid of hard work," she said, annoyed. Why was it that everyone was so negative about the place? "I happen to like old houses. There's plenty of room and it's quiet."

"Well, it's isolated enough," he agreed.

She'd heard enough. He must have sensed that he'd made her angry again.

"Look, I'm sorry. We really have gotten off on the wrong foot. Let me make it up to you."

"That's not necessary."

"No, give me a chance. I'm pretty good with a hammer."

She would hope so, given the logo on his truck. "I'm afraid I can't afford to hire anyone right now," she said, taken aback. She'd expected him to ask her to dinner again. Apparently he'd changed his mind about wanting a date with her.

"I wasn't looking for a job. Actually, I'm

taking some time off, but I thought maybe we could make a trade. As I said, I was looking for a place to board my horse while I'm here. I just thought maybe we could trade horse boarding for some part-time construction work. After all, I do owe you after last night."

"You don't owe me anything. I ended up with a very nice date last night. In fact, he was great."

Nate arched a brow. "Great, huh? Well, that *would* be hard to top. But was there any electricity involved?"

"I beg your pardon?"

"Did he offer to check your wiring?"

She had to smile. "As a matter of fact…no."

"I didn't think so."

She felt herself weaken. She definitely could use his expertise and she had plenty of room to board his horse. So what was the problem?

"Just think about my offer." He gave her a smile. What was it about that smile?

"I'll give it some thought." She took a step backward. "You're sure we've never met before?" she asked again.

"I'm sure. I would have remembered."

NATE REMEMBERED ONLY too well. And he figured it was just a matter of time before McKenna remembered, too. By then, he hoped, he'd be long gone.

"Nice horse," she said, giving Blue another pat before starting across the street.

He still couldn't believe Blue had taken a liking to her. She really *was* good with horses. He thought about her date last night and wondered who the man had been. He'd lied about seeing her with the man. Arlene had filled him in when she'd called this morning to offer to set him up with someone else.

A sliver of worry burrowed under his skin as he watched McKenna cross the street and considered what to do next. He had to find a way to spend more time at Harper House. As he climbed into his truck he looked in her direction again. She was standing in front of the hardware store, her blond hair floating around her shoulders, her Western hat brim low, so low he couldn't see those incredible blue eyes, but he could feel them on him.

Had she remembered where she'd seen him before? He would never forget the first time he'd seen her, sitting on her horse outside the fence at Harper House all those years ago. Had he known then that their paths would cross? Or had he only dreamed they would?

But not like this. Not with him lying to her.

He told himself he couldn't concern himself with anything but finishing what he'd come to Whitehorse to do. He couldn't let anyone get in his way. Not even McKenna Bailey. Especially McKenna Bailey.

Why the hell did she have to buy that house?

He shook his head as he started the engine and pulled away. As he drove down the main street he had that feeling again of being watched. Hadn't he figured he wasn't the only one who'd come back to Whitehorse after hearing of Ellis Harper's death? He was counting on company. What better place to settle old scores than Harper House, where it had all begun?

THE HOUSE FELT EVEN colder than before when McKenna unlocked the door and stepped inside. A weak June sun shone in the dirty windows. She climbed the stairs to the third floor and looked out to the spot where she had ridden as a young girl. She could imagine herself sitting astride her horse, staring up at the house.

This is where the boy she'd seen had been standing, looking out at her. She shivered, unable to shake the eerie feeling that came over her as she looked out.

Turning away from the window, she moved to the middle of the room and tried to visualize what it would look like cleaned up, painted, blinds on the windows.

It was going to take a lot of work, she thought, looking up at the bare lightbulb hanging down.

She really did need someone to look at the wiring.

Nate Dempsey had graciously offered to help. Why hadn't she accepted? She had plenty of space to board his horse, and trading for help around here would have been ideal.

But she knew why she'd hesitated. That nagging feeling that he wanted something from her. Something more than a place to board his horse. Or camp. What if he'd lied and he was the one who'd been digging on the hillside behind the house? But digging for what?

It made no sense for anyone to be digging out there. What could there possibly have been buried behind the house?

It wasn't as if there was buried treasure out there. Ellis Harper hadn't had two nickels to scrape together. Or had he? He wouldn't be the first old-timer to hide money in the yard. He might not even have remembered he'd done it.

McKenna thought of her grandmother, Nina Mae Cross, who had Alzheimer's. If she'd buried any money, she wouldn't remember doing it either.

Other than seeing Nate Dempsey ride away from Harper House and having him standing her up for a date, she wasn't sure what it was about him that made her leery of him. He seemed normal enough, and she did like his horse. And his smile was killer.

There was something about him that drew her to him, which made no sense, since Flynn Garrett was much better-looking and she hadn't felt anything but mild interest. Even his kiss hadn't set off a firecracker, let alone a Roman candle.

But Nate Dempsey… All he had to do was smile and it was the Fourth of July. She just wished she could remember where she'd seen him before. It would drive her crazy until she recalled.

She glanced around the room, realizing that her earlier enthusiasm for the house had waned some—and that worried her since so many people seemed to think she was crazy to try to save this house. She knew that her older sister, Eve, thought she'd acted impulsively.

Maybe she had. But even as a girl, sitting astride her horse and looking at the house from a distance, she'd had the feeling that the house needed her, that it called to her.

Well, what it was saying right now was that she'd made a mistake. Not that the property alone wasn't worth what she'd paid for the place. But she was beginning to fear that razing the house *was* the smartest thing to do.

It wasn't something she wanted to hear as she skirted the ancient square of linoleum that covered the center of the wood-plank floor like a rug. Stubbornness alone would make her try to save this house.

She noticed that the wood around the linoleum was in fair shape. Her first job would be to tear out the floor covering to expose the wood, she thought as she bent down to lift a corner of the linoleum.

One of the boards stuck to the underside. The board lifted a few inches, and she thought she saw something in the space beneath it. Sitting down on the floor, she shoved the floor covering back with her feet and pried the board the rest of the way up.

In the space between the floor joists was what had clearly been a child's secret hiding compartment. There were several old metal children's toys, rusted with age, a handful of marbles and a piece of rolled-up once-white paper.

She wiped away the cobwebs and plucked the faded paper from between the boards, letting the board and linoleum drop back down as she scooted out of the way.

Unrolling the paper, she thought she'd find a child's artwork. Instead it was an old announcement about Whitehorse Days, a June rodeo event held every year at the local fairgrounds. This one was dated twenty-one years ago.

Disappointed that's all it was, she turned the paper over. And froze.

Her pulse roared in her ears as she realized with horror what she had in her hands.

Chapter Six

The sheet of paper gripped in her fingers was stained dark with blood—bloody thumbprints and what appeared to be more than a half dozen names. Next to each small bloody thumbprint was a name and an age. All of them were children twelve and under.

But it was the wording at the top of the page, written in an older child's shaky print, that horrified her.

Under the threat of death we make a blood oath to avenge those who harmed us in this house if it is the last thing we ever do. We vow to return at a set time to finish what needs to be done—or suffer the consequences.

It sounded like something kids might write. But the bloody prints on it and the names and ages gave her chill.

She glanced around the room. What *had* happened in this house? Shivering, she scanned down the list of names.

Roy Vaughn
Lucky Thomas
Steven Cross
Bobby French
Andrew Charles
Denny Jones
Lyle Weston

She didn't recognize any of the names and was thankful for that. Seven names on the list. What had happened to these boys?

McKenna hadn't thought too much about it when Eve had told her that Harper House had been a home for troubled boys. It hadn't mattered. Now she wasn't so sure.

Under the threat of death? Suffer the consequences? Surely they were being overdramatic. Kids were like that. And yet, as she stared down at the paper, her hand trembled.

The boys had made a blood oath to avenge the people who'd hurt them. They'd spilled their own blood to make the vow.

The paper was dated twenty-one years ago. The boys who'd signed it were too young to do anything at the time. But they would all be in their late twenties to early thirties by now. If they really had planned to do something to the people they felt had mistreated them, wouldn't they have done it by now? Wouldn't she have heard about it?

Still, she felt the need to show this to someone. Her soon-to-be brother-in-law, the sheriff. Not her sisters. It would only upset them, just as it had her.

Carefully she rolled up the sheet and rose on quaking legs from the floor to put it in her large shoulder bag.

As she turned, she let out a shriek. A man she'd never seen before stood in the doorway. He was massive, his clothing worn, his expression amused.

"Did I frighten you?" he asked, knowing full well he had and seeming to enjoy her discomfort. "I called up from below. I guess you didn't hear me." He glanced toward her shoulder bag she was still holding after she'd stuck the paper inside. How long had he been standing there watching her?

"Can I help you?" she asked. Her voice quaked, giving away her fear at being alone here in the house with him. Why hadn't she heard him drive up?

"I was told in town that you needed some help out here," he said, glancing past her to the window. "I'm handy with tools." His gaze came back to her and she saw that odd amusement in his eyes.

"I'm sorry, but you were misinformed. I'm planning on doing the work myself," she said. "But thanks for the offer Mr...."

"Turner," he said. "Hal Turner."

The name was a lie. His gaze challenged her to call him on it. Just as it challenged her to shake his hand as he outstretched it toward her.

His slightly damp paw of a hand swallowed hers. She did her best not to grimace. "McKenna Bailey."

"I know who you are," he said as she broke contact and fought the urge to wipe her hand on her jeans.

He knew who she was? But she didn't know who *he* was. She took a step toward the door, but he was blocking her way.

"I work cheap," he said, not moving.

He knew he was scaring her. He seemed to be enjoying it. She tested the weight of her shoulder bag, the only weapon at her disposal. The purse, if swung hard enough, might surprise him but little more.

She had a fleeting crazy thought: if she'd agreed to let Nate Dempsey board his horse out here, he'd be here now.

The sound of a vehicle coming up her road made her almost sag with relief. The man heard it, too, and she saw his expression change.

"Well, if you're sure you don't need any help…" He turned and stepped back through the doorway.

She listened to his heavy footfalls on the stairs

and tried to calm down. The man had frightened her more than she wanted to admit.

Stepping to the window, she saw a pickup pull up in the yard and felt such a sense of relief she had to grab hold of the window frame to keep her knees from buckling.

Nate Dempsey's truck came to a stop next to her pickup. She saw with surprise that there were only two vehicles in the yard—her pickup and Nate's. How had the man who called himself Hal Turner gotten out here? And where was he now?

She watched Nate Dempsey emerge from the cab of his truck and stop to stare up at the house, his expression hidden in the shadow of his straw hat's brim.

The house suddenly felt ice-cold as she rushed to the north-side window. The backyard was empty. So was the hillside behind it. Was it possible the man had never left the house?

McKenna ran back to the front of the house to tap on the window. Nate looked up, shading his eyes. She waved, wanting him to know where she was just in case the man was still in the house. Waiting for her.

She ran downstairs, not stopping until she was through the front door and halfway down the porch steps.

THE MINUTE NATE SAW McKenna's face he knew something was wrong. She came rushing out of the house and down the porch steps. Her cheeks were flushed, her blue eyes wide and wild.

"Hey! You all right?"

"Sure." She tried to brush it off, but he saw the way she glanced around the yard, then looked over her shoulder back at the house as if she was being chased. "It's just that there was this man here…."

"Is he still in the house?" Nate asked, suddenly on alert.

"I don't know. Did you see anyone leave?"

"No. I'll make sure he's gone," he said as she hugged herself. She didn't seem to hear him. He touched her arm; it was ice-cold. "Just wait here."

He mounted the steps of the porch. He could feel the gun in his shoulder holster, snug against his side, as he opened the front door and listened for a moment before stepping inside.

The house seemed unusually quiet. He glanced back at McKenna. She was right where he'd left her. It took him only a few minutes to search the house since he knew all its hiding places. He started upstairs, working his way down. There was only one place he dreaded looking in.

The basement.

He hadn't been down there in more than twenty years, but he could remember it as if it were yesterday. The smell, the feel of the cold dampness around him, the furtive sounds that made his skin crawl.

At the door to the basement he hesitated, his hand inches from the knob. Funny how fears, no matter how irrational, linger into adulthood.

He opened the basement door. The smell alone was enough to transport him back. He was seven again, a skinny, scared kid locked in the basement for a punishment he didn't deserve.

He took a breath and reached around the edge of the doorjamb for the light switch.

McKenna had waited. Then, feeling vulnerable outside and worried about Nate, she'd cautiously climbed the porch steps and slipped back inside the house.

She saw him standing at the top of the stairs to the basement as if listening. She started to tell him where the light switch was, since it wasn't easy to find. But the words never left her lips as she watched him reach around the doorjamb and flip on the light as if he'd done it dozens of times.

Startled, for a moment she couldn't catch her breath. How had he known where the light switch was?

She realized even though he hadn't bid on the house, he'd probably toured it before the auction like everyone else. He would have remembered the location of the light switch just as she had.

She let out a ragged breath. Her heart was pounding and she knew she wasn't thinking clearly and hadn't been since she'd turned around to find that man standing in the bedroom doorway upstairs.

She listened to Nate descend the steps slowly, almost tentatively, and tried not to read any more into what she'd seen than she already had. There had been no Nate Dempsey on the list of names she'd found under the floorboards.

When he came back up a few moments later, moving a little quicker as he ascended the steps, she was waiting for him.

"I thought I told you to wait outside," he said, sounding irritated and upset, although she doubted it was with her. He apologized at once. "Sorry. I just wanted to make sure he wasn't still in the house."

She watched him switch off the light, then close the basement door. "Did you find anything?"

He shook his head, still seeming upset. "So tell me what happened."

She told him what she knew, which wasn't much. "He was large and unkempt."

"Homeless, you think?"

"Maybe. He said he'd heard I needed help with the house."

"Where would he have heard that?" Nate asked.

"Anywhere in town. News travels fast around Whitehorse. When I told him I didn't need any help, he kept at me. I tried to step past him, but he was blocking the door."

Nate swore. "When you're here alone, you really should lock your door."

"I've never locked my doors in my life in this part of Montana."

"Well, maybe you'd better start. So did this guy tell you what his name was or give you any idea what he wanted?"

"Just work, I assume. He said his name was Hal Turner, but I think he was lying." She couldn't miss Nate's reaction to the name. "Do you know him?"

"I used to know a Hal Turner, that's all."

That *wasn't* all. "Maybe it's the same guy."

Nate was shaking his head. "The Hal Turner I knew is dead."

That would explain his startled reaction, she told herself.

Nate seemed anxious and upset again. "You shouldn't stay out here alone. It's not safe."

"You think he'll come back?" She hated the catch she heard in her voice.

"If he thinks you're here alone, he will. A

woman alone this far from another house—you're a sitting duck."

"What would you have me do? This is going to be my home. I refuse to be run off. I'll get some pepper spray. I'll lock the doors. I'll be more careful."

He took off his Western straw hat and wiped his shirtsleeve over his face. She noticed he was sweating, while she was freezing.

"Think about my offer. Right now I'm staying at a motel in town, but I'd rather be camped somewhere. I could pitch my tent down by the creek. You wouldn't know I was there—unless you needed me." He held up a hand before she could say anything. "Just think about it. I'll check the barn and outbuildings to make sure he's not hiding out there." He didn't wait for a response.

She stood at the back screen door, hugging herself as she watched him cut across the yard, toward the barn. In all the years she'd lived up here she'd never been afraid. Until now.

But she wasn't going to let one incident like this make her frightened. She would take more precautions. Once she was moved in she didn't expect any trouble.

Not that she didn't realize how close she'd come. What would she have done if Nate hadn't stopped by? She hated to think what would have happened.

Why had he come by? she wondered, frowning. She hadn't even thought to ask.

WHEN NATE RETURNED to the house, he noticed the change in McKenna. She was acting skittish, and he realized she was probably picking up on his reaction. But what she'd told him had frightened him more than he wanted to admit.

At first he'd thought the man had been just some homeless poor soul passing through town, probably looking for work or a free meal, who'd come on a little too strong and had frightened her.

Until she'd said the man had called himself Hal Turner. Nate hadn't heard that name in years. But he would never forget it. Hal Turner hadn't just been one of the first boys to live in Harper House, he had become a hero to the boys who came later.

It was Hal Turner who'd started the first revenge pact among the boys. Allegedly he'd grown up and come back to Whitehorse as part of that original pact to kill the first Harper House attendants: Norman and Alma Cherry. At least that was the story. Hal Turner had allegedly made the murders look like a murder/suicide and gotten away with it.

Coincidence that someone showed up now using that name?

Not in a million years.

The man who'd called himself Hal Turner hadn't come looking for work. Nor had it been about McKenna. No, the man had been sending a message. And the message was for Nate.

"Are you all right?" he asked McKenna, worried that he'd done something to give himself away. Or, maybe worse, that she remembered where she'd seen him before.

She nodded, looking scared again.

"Look," he said. "I understand if you don't want me staying out here. Forget I said anything about it. Same with boarding my horse or me helping with the house. I tend to come on too strong sometimes."

"No, I appreciate the offer. It's just that I can't ask you to—"

"You're not *asking*. The truth is, I'm picky about where I leave Blue. He's temperamental with most people, and after seeing how he took to you I just thought…"

He saw her consider. The horse, he thought, was his ticket.

"Let me give it some thought," she said. "I do appreciate the offer. I don't know what I would have done if you hadn't shown up when you did."

"No problem."

"Thank you." She brushed a lock of blond hair back from her face, and he could tell the man who'd been here earlier had made her feel vulnerable—something new for McKenna Bailey.

"Are you having second thoughts about the house?" he asked.

"*No.*" She softened the abrupt answer with a smile. "The house apparently has a past, one that the locals think precludes anyone living here—maybe especially me."

"What kind of past?" he asked, although he knew only too well.

"It was some kind of boys' ranch for troubled youth years ago," she said. "I think the boys might have been abused."

"What makes you think that?" He warned himself to be careful. He was on shaky ground.

"Just things I've heard," she said noncommittally. "You don't seem surprised by that."

He shrugged. "I heard some rumors."

"You don't think they're true?"

He caught the hint of hopefulness. She wanted him to tell her nothing horrible had happened in this house. He wished he could. Not even he could lie that well.

"It was a long time ago, right?" he said and narrowed his gaze at her, only half kidding when he asked, "You're not worried that the house might be haunted, are you?"

"I don't believe in any of that nonsense. I just feel badly for the boys."

He wondered if she would if she knew some of them. It wasn't just ghosts that came back to haunt a place.

"I wish I could find out if any of them survived what happened to them here," she said wistfully. "It would make me feel better."

He doubted that a whole lot. "I can't see that it could make any difference when it comes to this house. You can't change the past."

"I suppose not," she agreed.

He studied her. The house was getting to her. "You can always unload it if you change your mind about living here."

"Is that what you would do?" she asked, her gaze intent on him again.

"It's not *my* house."

She turned to the window, staring out as if she could see the boys out there in the yard, before she turned to him abruptly. "You never said why you stopped out when you did."

He could see that she was still guarded with him. He said the first thing that came to his mind. He'd come out here hoping she wouldn't be around so he could look the place over again in the daylight. Digging was out of the question— except at night, when no one was around.

"I nearly forgot," he said, winging it. "Everyone in town is talking about something called White-horse Days? I suppose you've been?"

"Whitehorse Days?" she repeated, her face seeming paler than before, the light dusting of freckles popping out like stars on a clear night.

He knew then that she'd found the blood oath that Roy Vaughn had made everyone sign. He had wondered if it still existed. He swore silently. The damned thing had everyone's names on it. Well, almost everyone's.

"I heard it's a fun time," he said, rattled by the realization. No wonder she had looked so spooked.

"If you like cotton candy and carnival rides and farm animals and baked-goods contests."

"Do you like that sort of thing?"

She seemed surprised. She let out a small laugh. "Actually, I do."

He knew she was waiting for him to ask her out. Hell, he almost did. What was he thinking? Instead he turned at the sound of a vehicle pulling up in the drive. "Appears you have company. I saw some wiring coming into the house that looked kind of funky. I was just going to take a quick look. Wouldn't want the place to catch fire and burn down." No, wouldn't want that.

He ducked out the back door, surprised how much making a date with her to Whitehorse Days appealed to him. But what would have been the point? He'd either be finished here and long gone by then…

…or he'd be dead.

Chapter Seven

McKenna looked out to see a pickup she recognized pull into the drive. Eve was behind the wheel, Faith in the passenger seat. McKenna had never been so happy to see her sisters.

She felt off balance. First the man who'd called himself Hal Turner and then Nate Dempsey almost asking her for a date. Or had she just imagined that?

Worse, she was seriously considering taking him up on his offer—not just a trade for work on the house but his staying out by the creek that meandered through the property. Until she moved in, at least. Someone to watch the place.

Glancing back through the house, she caught a glimpse of Nate. He appeared to be doing just what he'd said—checking the wiring to the house. She felt a wave of gratitude that was quickly replaced with concern.

Maybe he was just who he seemed to be—a

nice man who wanted to help her. Why did that alone make her suspicious of him?

Because he wanted more. She could feel it, and her instincts told her what he wanted had something to do with this house. And yet she was about to invite him to camp by the creek? Had she lost her mind?

Maybe, she thought as she turned and walked through the house to meet her sisters. Or maybe what bothered her was that she couldn't remember where she'd seen him before.

"Boy, are you a welcome sight!" she called from the porch as her sisters climbed out of the pickup carrying cleaning supplies.

"Are you all right?" Eve asked as McKenna came down the porch steps to help carry the supplies.

"Great. I'm just glad to see you," she said.

"We figured you could use all the help you could get," Faith was saying.

"You have company?" Eve was studying Nate's pickup as if memorizing the license plate number.

"Not company exactly," McKenna said as Nate Dempsey rounded the outside corner of the house.

He gave her a nod as he saw that she had guests. "It's going to need a little work, but there's nothing to worry about for now. Catch you later," he said as he climbed into his pickup.

"Just a minute!" McKenna called to him. "I need to tell him something," she said to her sisters before hurrying over to his pickup.

He had his window down and looked surprised but glad she'd come over.

"I just wanted to tell you," she said, a little breathless, more from her concern about what she was about to do than the short run. "I'd like to take you up on your offer. For a while."

"You're sure?" he asked, his expression serious.

"Yes. I'd appreciate it. If you can get the shower to work downstairs, by the kitchen, you can use that bathroom."

He smiled. "I'd planned to use the outhouse behind the barn and bathe in the creek."

"That won't be necessary. Bring your horse and you're welcome to stay in the house if you like until I get moved in."

"No. I'd just as soon camp by the creek. But I might take you up on the use of the shower. Thanks."

"Thank *you*," McKenna said and stepped back from the pickup as he cranked up the engine.

"What was that about?" Eve asked as McKenna joined her again.

"Nate's a contractor."

Eve watched him drive away. "I didn't know you were going to hire a contractor."

"I'm not. He's interested in trading his services for boarding his horse out here." She left out the part about him camping in her backyard.

"Are you going to do it?" Eve asked, sounding surprised.

"Yeah," McKenna said. "I could use the help and I like his horse."

Eve raised a brow. "His horse? How did you meet this man? Not through Arlene's Internet dating service, I hope."

McKenna laughed as if that was the craziest thing she'd ever heard. "If Arlene had found him, she'd be convinced he was perfect for me. Don't you want to hear about my date last night with the cowboy who bid against me for the house?"

"Seriously?" Faith cried.

"Seriously. He is handsome as all get-out, too. He bought champagne so we could celebrate me beating him. We had a steak dinner and he even kissed me good night." McKenna knew she was going on too much in her effort to divert interest away from Nate Dempsey.

Eve was eyeing her suspiciously. Her older sister knew her too well. "So let's see this place you bought," she said, glancing skeptically at the house.

"I want to know more about the cowboy hunk you had a date with last night," Faith said.

"His name's Flynn Garrett and he loves horses."

"He sounds perfect for you," Faith said as they headed for the house.

Not really, McKenna thought as she glanced down the road. All she could see was the dust Nate Dempsey's pickup had churned up into the warm summer air.

"The house is certainly big enough," Faith said as she stepped into the shadow of the house.

"Three stories," McKenna agreed, glancing upward.

"Isn't it scary out here alone?" Faith asked.

Recently? Yes. "It won't be once I get moved in." Not to mention Nate Dempsey would be camped down by the creek. At least for a while.

"It's pretty scary-looking in the daylight," Faith said. "I can't imagine staying out here at night."

Would everyone please just stop it!

Eve shot their younger sister a warning look. "I'm sure it will be fine once McKenna gets her horses out here. And, anyway, we're just a few miles down the road."

McKenna gave her older sister a grateful smile. She needed to hear that right now. Eve had lived alone. True, her house had been broken into and a crazy woman had almost killed her….

Pushing those thoughts aside, she and Eve climbed the porch steps after Faith, who was already letting the screen door slam behind her in her rush to see the house.

"I should warn you—it's still a mess in there," McKenna called after her.

"You sure you're all right?" Eve whispered, grabbing her arm to detain her for a moment.

McKenna realized that Faith's question about being scared out here had her hugging herself tightly. "It's just cold in the house, that's all."

Eve nodded skeptically as they followed Faith inside the house. Eve stopped at once, looking back over her shoulder at McKenna as if even more worried.

As McKenna was hit by a wall of heat, she understood why. The house was scorching hot, the sun blinding as it bore through the dusty windows, and no breath of air moved inside the four walls.

"I can't tell you how much I appreciate your help cleaning this place," McKenna said, changing the subject. "I'm hoping to start painting upstairs tomorrow so I can get moved in."

"I guess we'll start upstairs, then," Eve said. "It's good Ellis Harper's cousin Anita Samuelson hired someone to clean out all the junk before you bought the place. I heard Ellis was a terrible pack rat. Every inch of this house was filled."

McKenna thought about the secreted paper she'd discovered under the floorboards, but she wasn't about to mention it to Eve or Faith. They were worried enough about her living in this place. And, anyway, hadn't she convinced herself there was nothing to it after all these years?

NATE DEMPSEY KNEW the moment he opened his motel room door that he wasn't alone. It was something he'd learned at a young age, an awareness of his surroundings that had saved his life on more than one occasion.

He stepped in, moving quickly to the side to avoid being framed in the doorway and made into an easy target. At the same time he drew the gun from his shoulder holster. The movement was practiced and smooth. If he'd ever needed the gun, it was in Whitehorse, he thought, ironically a town with almost no crime.

"Easy," said a voice from the shadows. "No need for that."

Nate recognized the slightly amused voice as Lucky Thomas stepped from behind the bathroom door.

Two things struck Nate in that instant. Lucky had changed little from the good-looking kid he'd been. And Nate had seen Lucky recently—at the auction. Only he hadn't recognized him because he'd never gotten a clear view of him. But even after twenty-one years the way the man moved had seemed familiar.

It hadn't registered that the man at the auction

might be Lucky Thomas. Probably because this was the last place Nate had expected to see him.

"What the hell are you doing here?" Nate demanded as he holstered his weapon.

"Nice to see you, too," Lucky said, clasping Nate's hand to pull him into a hug. "It's been too long."

Nate nodded as he stepped back to look at Lucky. Nate had been seven, Lucky nine, when they'd met at Harper House.

"*You're* awfully jumpy," Lucky said. "And packin' heat, too."

Nate swore. "What *are* you doing here?"

"Isn't it obvious?" Lucky said. "I heard about Ellis Harper dying. I knew you'd come up here. I figured you'd need someone to watch your back."

Did Lucky know that Roy Vaughn was in town? Or had he just assumed Roy would come back because of that stupid oath they'd taken?

Nate shook his head. He'd never expected to see Lucky again after the state had come and taken them away in separate cars.

"Twenty-one years," Lucky said as if thinking the same thing. He dropped into a chair at the small round table next to the closed drapes, pulled a flask from his jacket pocket and offered it to Nate.

Nate shook his head as he pulled out the other chair, drawing it back so he could stretch out his long legs.

"Just being here brings it all back, doesn't it?"

"Yeah," Nate agreed. Not that the nightmares had ever gone very far away.

"Can you believe old man Harper hung in all these years?" Lucky asked.

"Why the hell did you bid on Harper House?"

Lucky laughed. "I got a little carried away."

"What would you have done if you'd won the bid?" Nate had to ask.

Lucky shrugged. "I had this crazy idea that I could buy the place and burn that hellhole down. I guess I can still do that, only it won't be my house I'm burning down," he added with a laugh.

Nate said nothing, fearing that Lucky meant what he said about planning to burn down the house. It was a strange feeling knowing someone so well for such a short period of time. He still felt he knew him.

But how was that possible? He hadn't seen Lucky in years, didn't know what had happened to him. If they hadn't both come back because of Ellis Harper's death, they probably would never have crossed paths again.

Hell, Nate didn't even know Lucky's real name. From the day the scrawny, good-looking kid had arrived at Harper House he'd said to call him Lucky Thomas, as if it was an inside joke that only he could appreciate.

"I could have bought the house, you know,"

Lucky said. "I have the money." He shrugged. "So tell me you're not here because of the pact."

Nate shook his head. "That was just kids pretending to be tough."

"Right. You just keep telling yourself that, but don't expect me to believe it. Roy Vaughn seemed pretty serious the night he made us all sign it. Well, almost all of us." He grinned at Nate. "They'll all be afraid not to come."

"Is that why you're here?" Nate asked.

Lucky laughed. "To fulfill my...obligations? That's it. But you," he said, studying Nate, "I figure you've got bigger fish to fry than killing some mean old people. I heard Frank Merkel and Rosemarie Blackmore are still kicking. Hard to believe. I thought they were ancient when we were boys. Apparently no one has tipped them over yet. So what can I do to help?"

Nate watched Lucky take another drink from the flask, then screw the lid back on and put it into his jacket pocket again. "Go home."

Lucky laughed. "You don't even know where my home *is*."

"No, I don't. Just so long as it's away from Whitehorse—and Harper House."

"Here's the way I figure it," Lucky said. "Whatever you have planned, it's dangerous or you wouldn't be packin'. Add to that the fact that you're doing nothing to hide. In fact, just the opposite. It's almost as if you're looking for trouble."

Lucky knew him better than even Nate had thought.

"I, on the other hand, don't really want to stick my neck out," Lucky said with a grin. "So I'm sneaking into your motel room and planning to sneak right back out."

"Good. Sneak right back out of town. This doesn't concern you."

Lucky laughed. "Everything about Harper House concerns me." He seemed to search Nate's face. "I can't believe you're still looking for Johnny."

Nate remembered the feeling he'd had that he was being watched while digging for Johnny's body. He'd thought it was Roy Vaughn. But maybe it had been Lucky.

"And not just Johnny. If the gun is any indication, you're still looking for Roy Vaughn."

"Like I said, this doesn't concern you. I know what I'm doing." Right now Nate wouldn't put money on that, but he didn't want to talk about Johnny. Even after all these years it still hurt too much.

"So you think Roy Vaughn will come back," Lucky said.

"He already has," Nate said. Only he was calling himself Hal Turner and making no secret out of why he was in town.

Chapter Eight

By late afternoon McKenna's sisters had left, after helping her clean, promising to come back the next morning to paint.

She waited until they'd driven away before she locked the front door and went to the back of the house. Stepping out, she surveyed the yard for tracks.

It still bothered her. Where had the man who called himself Hal Turner gone? Or, more to the point, how had he gotten out here? Harper House was a long way from town, and no one had seen him leave.

It made her uneasy even though she knew that Nate had searched all the outbuildings as well as the house. Since then, she'd made a point of locking the doors.

Out back, the ground close to the house was still damp from a rain earlier in the week. She could make out boot prints in the soft soil where

Nate Dempsey had checked the wiring coming into the house. Along with his tracks were a set of others, these larger and made by cheap work boots.

She shuddered, her blood running cold as she saw where the man had stood beneath the back windows. There were handprints on the glass where he had wiped the dust to peer inside.

Nearby were Nate's Western boot tracks. Nate had to have seen where the man had looked in the window. No wonder he'd been so worried about her staying out here alone.

Inside the house, she locked the back door and stood for a moment leaning against it. Her heart was racing. She'd never felt afraid in all the years she'd lived in this isolated country.

But today she was running scared. The man had frightened her. As had the document the boys had signed with bloody fingerprints. She shuddered at the memory, although common sense told her that nothing had come of it.

She was just thankful that she'd had the good sense to ask Nate Dempsey to stay by the creek. It was still a good way from the house, but if she needed him, she could reach him a lot faster than getting anyone out here from Old Town or Whitehorse.

She reminded herself that Nate Dempsey wouldn't always be around. If she was going to live here, she had to come to grips with the house's past and the remoteness of the property. She refused to live in fear.

She started for the front door, when she realized she'd left her shoulder bag with the paper the boys had signed upstairs on the third floor. She'd dropped it after the man had left, to wave down at Nate in the front yard.

Climbing the stairs, she quickly retrieved her bag. While she'd pretty much convinced herself there was nothing to the document she'd found, she still wanted to show it to Sheriff Carter Jackson.

As she turned to go back downstairs, she caught sight of movement behind her. She let out a yelp before she realized it had only been a cat.

A black cat. Good thing she wasn't superstitious. But how had it gotten into the house?

On seeing her, the cat turned and raced down the stairs. She followed. The moment she opened the front door the cat took off across the porch to disappear in the higher weeds along the side of the house.

It must have been Ellis Harper's cat. She'd have to pick up some cat food in town for it. Or maybe it was Ethel Winthrop's up the road. Just the thought of Ethel reminded her of the woman's warning about buying this house.

ARLENE EVANS COULDN'T have been more excited to have a new client for her rural online dating service—and one her age, to boot. Not only that, Hank Monroe seemed to think Arlene was the cat's pajamas—an expression her mother had used but one that fit.

Hank Monroe was something, that was for sure. It still amazed her how much respect he seemed to have for her as a woman—and as a business-woman.

"This online rural dating thing you started, why, it's brilliant," Hank had said when they'd talked earlier on the phone.

He'd called to say he'd made reservations for dinner at Northern Lights restaurant at seven and that he'd pick her up at six so they could take a ride beforehand.

Her ex-husband Floyd hadn't been the least bit impressed when she'd started the business. Nor had he ever taken her out to dinner at such a nice restaurant. Floyd always said it was cheaper to eat at home.

After dinner they were going to the movie. There was only one showing in Whitehorse at the old-time theater, and she didn't even care what was showing. She felt like a girl again, all starry-eyed and giggly.

Hank hadn't suggested that she make popcorn to sneak into the show to save money, the way

Floyd would have. She was betting Hank Monroe wouldn't be cheap about beverages or candy at the movie, either.

But even if Hank Monroe had been flat broke, she would have liked him. He made her laugh. He made her forget that most of her life had been dismal at best. He made her feel special.

Arlene knew she shouldn't be thinking this way, but Hank Monroe gave her something she hadn't had for a long, long time. Hope. Hope for the future—something she sorely needed given her disappointing offspring. Charlotte got more pregnant each day, her body grotesquely swollen, her once-pretty blond hair drab and lanky. Bo was either in front of the television or in his room, the stereo blaring.

Eventually Hank would want to meet her children.

Arlene Evans dreaded that day and planned to put it off as long as possible. She still held out hope that Charlotte would come to her senses and give the baby she was carrying up for adoption. Or at least give up the name of the married man who'd fathered the baby so he could be held responsible for child support if the fool girl decided to keep the infant once it was born.

Charlotte hadn't taken any interest in the baby books Arlene had bought for her. Half the time Arlene suspected her youngest daughter ignored the pregnancy, refusing to think about the fact that it was inevitably going to end in a baby.

Not that Arlene didn't know who would end up raising the baby if Charlotte insisted on keeping it. While it would be her first grandbaby, Arlene wasn't sure she was up to the task of raising another child. Look how her other children had turned out.

Nor did she have the time or patience for her own grown children—let alone a baby. It frightened her to think of what would happen to the infant under Charlotte's care. The girl wasn't even able to take care of herself.

That's why spending time with Hank Monroe was such a godsend. For a while Arlene could forget about her real life.

Unfortunately real life became realer by the day. Charlotte would be having her baby in less than a month. There was talk of Violet getting out of the mental institution. Bo was making no move toward leaving the nest.

Arlene had lived long enough to know that even a hint of happiness from her would attract disaster like a lightning rod in a storm.

It was only a matter of time before disaster struck. But in the meantime Arlene Evans was going to enjoy this fleeting feeling of being happy for the first time in her life.

NATE HADN'T RETURNED as far as McKenna knew, and she hated the worried feeling that gave her. She looked out the back window as she came downstairs, wondering where he'd gone—and if he'd even be back. He seemed a man who spurned ties. Or maybe he just wanted to keep his distance from her. Why did she care one way or the other?

She didn't know the man, wasn't sure she entirely trusted him…and yet she felt drawn to him. Just as she had at Harper House, she reminded herself. So why, since he seemed to have no real interest in her, was he planning to stay behind her house?

Because he was just a nice guy.

Or because his real interest was in her house?

Unable to stop herself, she went downstairs and stepped outside to see if he'd come back while she'd been upstairs working. It would be just like him to settle in back there without letting her know he'd returned.

But there was no pickup by the barn. No tent that she could see pitched beside the creek under the big cottonwoods.

As she started to go back into the house, she saw something that stopped her. That was odd. It almost looked as if someone had been digging up the hillside again. They'd clearly tried to cover it up, but the wind had blown off the weeds covering the spot.

She felt a chill. Who was doing this? Nate? Or someone else? Well, once he was staying back here, that should put an end to the digging, right? Maybe she should do some digging herself and see exactly what was back there.

Suddenly she didn't want to work any more today. She was feeling antsy and out of sorts and hated the reason why. It had bugged her all afternoon. Earlier she'd thought Nate was going to ask her out. But he hadn't.

He had made no effort to ask her out since he'd stood her up for their one and apparently only date. She told herself she didn't want to go out with him anyway, but still it bothered her that he hadn't even tried to make up for their date that never happened.

Because he wasn't interested in her. He was interested in her property. For a place to camp and board his horse. Nothing more.

She locked up the house and headed for her pickup feeling lost. It was too early to go to the ranch house. Faith probably would be in town with friends. McKenna hated the thought of wandering around her family's empty ranch house thinking about Nate Dempsey and this darned house.

As she climbed into her truck, she remembered the black cat she'd seen. Maybe it did belong to Ethel Winthrop up the road. McKenna knew she was only using the cat as an excuse to visit the elderly couple.

What she really wanted to do was ask about Harper House. Ethel had indicated at the auction that she knew things about the house, things McKenna needed to know.

Maybe it was time she knew what those things were.

A few miles up the road to the north, McKenna pulled into the Winthrop ranch and cut the pickup's engine. The breeze as she opened her truck door smelled of the thick stand of cotton-woods that ran along the creek behind the ranch house. The same creek that cut through her property.

Cows milled in a rich green pasture that ran as far as the eye could see. Only the blue-gray outline of the Little Rocky Mountains broke the long line of the horizon. The mountains and the badlands in the distance that marked the Missouri River gorge.

Ethel answered the door at McKenna's knock with a look of confusion. "Yes?"

"Hi, we met the other day. I'm McKenna Bailey. I bought the house down the road."

Ethel frowned, and McKenna was beginning to worry that this trip had been a waste of time when Ethel's husband, Edgar, came out of the kitchen.

"Who's here, Ethel?" he asked.

"I don't know," the elderly woman said vaguely.

"Why, it's the woman who bought Harper House," Edgar said. His wife started as if prodded with a cattle prod.

"*You!*" she said and stepped back, eyes widening with fear. "Have you heard the noises yet?"

"Ethel, let our guest come inside," Edgar said. "It's hot out there."

McKenna stepped into the cool, dim house. "Actually, I came about a cat I saw. Do you have a black cat?"

Ethel crossed herself. "There's no black cats on this ranch."

"Then it must have belonged to Ellis Harper," McKenna said quickly. "I'll see that it gets fed. But I *am* interested in knowing more about Harper House."

"A little late for that," Ethel said with a shake of her head.

"Ethel, didn't I see that you made some iced tea earlier?" her husband asked pointedly.

Ethel, distracted by the mention of the tea, padded off toward the kitchen.

"Won't you sit down?" he offered McKenna as he drew her into the living room. "You'll have to excuse my wife. She's been upset ever since you bought the house, worried about you living there alone."

"I haven't actually moved in yet," McKenna said as she took a seat on the flowered couch, moving one of a dozen pillows all adorned with yarn cross-stitch cat images.

"My wife likes cats," he said unnecessarily. "Just not black ones. She's superstitious that way."

McKenna smiled.

"You sure you want to go digging into the past?" he asked, glancing toward the kitchen.

McKenna could hear the clink of glasses, then the refrigerator open and close.

"Yes, I'm sure," she said, not sure at all. She owned the house. What did it matter now? Unless there was cause for concern because of the bloody document she'd found. Otherwise there was nothing to be done about the way the boys had been treated—or mistreated—at Harper House so many years ago.

Ethel called from the kitchen and Edgar rose to go help her. They both returned a few moments later with him carrying the tray. Ethel wrung her hands, winding them in the front of her apron as she looked nervously at McKenna.

"You sit there, Ethel," he said, directing his wife into a rocker as he put the tray on the coffee table and poured her a glass of iced tea, then another for McKenna before pouring one for himself.

The glass was cold and wet—and she wondered if she would ever be warm again.

"Did he tell you about the first Harper who owned the house?" Ethel demanded.

"I haven't told her anything," he said patiently. "I was waiting until you could join us. As you know how it works around these parts, the house keeps the name of whoever lived there first, so it's always been known as the Harper House."

Ethel hadn't touched her iced tea. "The first Harper? His wife died, and he died of a broken heart right after that. The house is unlucky."

Edgar sighed. "I think she's interested in the house's more recent history."

McKenna took a drink of her tea. It was cold and bitter.

"Those poor children who lived in that house?" Ethel touched the tiny cross she wore around her neck. "It was just horrible. When the wind blew out of the east we could hear them at night. The cries were unbearable."

"I called the sheriff a few times, but when he drove out, he'd never find anything amiss."

"Didn't look very hard, did he?" Ethel leaned toward McKenna conspiratorially. "He was like a lot of people who weren't concerned about what happened to those boys. Rough bunch. Most people were afraid of them and glad the people who ran Harper House kept the boys on the place."

"Didn't the boys tell the sheriff what was going on out there?" McKenna asked.

Edgar shook his head. "I would imagine they were afraid to say anything, swore everything was fine, poor things. A mismatched bunch they were, too. Orphans, strays, boys nobody wanted. It was a blessing when the state closed down the place."

McKenna felt sick. "When was that?"

Edgar gave that some thought. "Place ran from the seventies to sometime in the late eighties. Closed in 1987."

Twenty-one years ago, McKenna thought with a shudder.

"After that, Ellis Harper, a shirttail relative of the first Harper, came back and lived alone in the house until he died," Edgar said.

"The place drove him insane," Ethel said. "The ghosts of those boys. I stopped by to see him one day. He told me he'd seen two of them boys in the backyard. That old mutt he had kept barking and barking from the back steps as if he saw them, too, up on that hillside. But there wasn't anybody out there." She shook her head ruefully.

Edgar chuckled. "Hard to say what Ellis saw. He drank. That's what killed him," he said as if that explained seeing ghosts in the backyard.

"Did he ever mention any of the boys by name?" McKenna asked.

Ethel shook her head. "He just said 'them two' like they were the ones who haunted him. It gave me the shivers the way he said it, sounded as if he was half-afraid of them."

"Any chance Ellis might have buried money in the backyard?" she asked, trying out one theory.

Edgar chuckled.

"That's ridiculous," Ethel said. "If there is anything buried in that backyard, it's those boys."

McKenna couldn't suppress a shudder even though Edgar signaled with a shake of his head not to believe Ethel. "What *did* happen to the boys?"

"After the state closed the place, they took them," he said. "The younger ones were probably adopted. The older ones..." He shrugged. "The state saw that they were taken care of, I assume."

"Couldn't have come to any good, not after what they'd been through," Ethel said.

McKenna shared the woman's fear. "Would you recognize any of them if you saw them?"

Both Edgar and Ethel shook their heads. "Never got a good look at any of them, and after all these years..." Edgar sighed. "I wouldn't worry about them. They're men now. They either put their pasts behind them or they didn't."

"Well, thank you for the tea and the information," she said, putting her glass down on the coffee table to leave even though she'd barely touched her tea.

"That house is evil. You'd be wise to strike a match to it," Ethel said.

"I don't believe houses are evil—just people," McKenna said.

Ethel gave her a we'll-see-about-that look as McKenna left. She was still disturbed by what she'd learned about the house but somewhat relieved. If the state had stepped in, the boys would have been saved and could have gone on to lead normal lives—she hoped. At any rate, the boys had apparently put Harper House and the blood oath and their plans for revenge behind them.

It was near dark by the time she reached the road to her house. She would make a point of bringing what she needed tomorrow so she could start staying in the house. She wasn't going to let anyone scare her off her own property. Especially ghosts.

But as she started to drive by her new house she remembered that she'd forgotten her paint samples upstairs in the third-floor bedroom. How foolish of her not to have gotten the paint samples at the same time she'd grabbed her purse. She'd also apparently left the light on when she'd gone back up to get her shoulder bag.

Or maybe Nate had turned on the light.

As she pulled into the drive, though, she was disappointed to see that Nate's pickup was nowhere in sight. Was it possible he'd changed his mind about staying out here? She tried to remember turning on the light upstairs.

Earlier, with everyone in the house working, she'd felt safe and excited. She'd thrown off her worry about the house being a mistake for a while. Cleaned, the rooms had taken on new life. She couldn't wait to see paint on the walls—starting with that front bedroom on the third floor. That would be her office.

She'd picked a nice sunny yellow to cover the drab faded blue in the room. A boy's room, she thought as she got out of her pickup.

The house loomed up out of the darkness, a black silhouette of jagged corners and cornices—except for the dim yellow light coming from the third-floor bedroom.

She hesitated for a moment, overwhelmed by everything the Winthrops had told her, finding the bloody document, being frightened by the man who'd called himself Hal Turner.

Reassuring herself that he was long gone—just like all the bad things that had happened here—she headed for the house, keys in hand, trying to remember if she'd locked the front door or not.

She hated being afraid. In order to live out here by herself and raise horses, she had to overcome these fears.

But she knew it wasn't ghosts that made her fingers tremble as she unlocked the front door and reached for the light switch. It was a fear that whatever horrors had happened in this house would act like a magnet to attract new evil as they did in those scary movies she'd watched with her sister Faith.

As she climbed the stairs to the third floor she told herself that kind of thinking was crazier than believing in ghosts. Dormant evil attracting evil. *Really.*

When she reached the third floor, the glow of the light spilled across the hardwood floor of the landing. She hesitated, positive she hadn't left the light on.

Taking a step toward the room, she started, her hand going to her mouth as she saw someone standing at the dormer-side window. Her breath caught in her throat and it was all she could do not to cry out.

But it wasn't a man next to the window. It was her sister Faith's jacket that she'd hung on what was left of the curtain rod.

The paint samples were on the windowsill where she'd left them. She hurried over and picked them up, hating how anxious she was to leave. *Once I have new locks and am moved in it will feel different. Once I have my horses out here, it'll be all right.*

As she turned out the light and started down the stairs, she heard a soft thump downstairs.

She froze, one foot balancing on a step, her hand gripping the wood railing. Listening, she heard the wind in the cottonwoods and the soft scrape of what had to be a limb against the side of the house.

Once she lived here she would get use to the house's noises, she told herself as she let out the breath she'd been holding and continued on down the stairs.

She tried not to hurry, telling herself this wasn't like her, turning on lights as she went and turning them off behind her. Down the stairs, through the living room, locking the door behind her as she crossed the porch and dropped down the stairs.

She didn't scare easily. But after the day she'd had— She tried to reassure herself. Her family ranch was only a few miles down the road. This was her country, her land. There was nothing to fear.

Something hit her the minute she reached the last porch step. What felt like a hand slammed into her back, and she went sprawling into the weeds, the air knocked from her.

For a moment she was too surprised to do anything more than gasp for breath. Then she was up, scrambling to her feet, running as fast as she could toward her pickup. She didn't dare look behind her. She knew it was the man who'd called himself Hal Turner. She knew he was right behind her, breathing down her neck, and that any moment he was going to grab her and—

She reached the pickup, flung open the door and dived inside, slamming the door behind her and hitting the locks. She was shaking all over as she looked out the windshield. Darkness cloaked the house and trees, deep shadows stretching across the yard. A breeze stirred the cottonwoods in a flicker of light and dark.

Where was he?

She fumbled the key into the ignition. The engine roared. She snapped on the headlights, bracing herself for when he came at her again. In her imagination she could see him coming at the truck with something to shatter the side window and grab her before she could—

Her mind raced as she shifted the pickup into First, wanting only to get out of there. She was trembling with fear—and confusion. Someone had pushed her down. She'd felt the hand in the middle of her back. A hard shove that had sent her sprawling.

But if the person had meant to harm her, why hadn't he come after her?

She hadn't imagined being pushed. She hadn't. But where had he gone. And why—

Suddenly her pickup cab was filled with the glare of a set of headlights as a vehicle came rushing toward her.

Chapter Nine

As his headlights splashed over McKenna's pickup, Nate Dempsey watched her kill her engine. He saw her hurrying to get the pickup going again, only to back into one of the fence posts.

He slowed, wondering what the hell was going on. Stopping his truck and horse trailer in the beams of her headlights, he climbed out, leaving his engine running, and walked cautiously through the glare of her headlights toward her.

When he reached the side of the pickup, he could see her face behind the wheel. It looked stark white, her blue eyes round as tumbleweeds. Both hands were gripping the wheel, and it seemed to take her a few moments before she recognized him. What had happened?

As he tapped on her side window, it came partway down and he caught a whiff of her perfume. It mingled with another smell he recognized at once. Fear.

"Are you all right?" he asked, seeing that she wasn't. Worse, she seemed afraid of him.

Her eyes flooded with tears, her voice breaking as she stared at him. "Someone was here. He… struck me."

"Are you hurt?"

She shook her head. "I don't know where he went."

His gaze went to the house. "I'll make sure he's gone."

"No," she cried. "He's dangerous."

If her attacker was who Nate believed it to be, the man was more than dangerous. He was a cold-blooded killer. "Lock your doors. Honk if you need me. I'll be right back."

He turned and left before she could argue further. Once out of the sweeping glow of the pickup's headlights, he pulled the gun from his shoulder holster and moved cautiously toward the house.

First he checked the area around the house, then made sure the doors were locked before he holstered the gun again and went back to her.

He was glad to see that she'd done what he'd told her to do. As he neared her pickup, she put her window down partway again, as if not sure who she had to fear.

"Feeling better?" he asked. He could see that she was. There were no more tears and she seemed to have steadied herself. He wasn't surprised given what he knew about her.

"Did you see him?"

Nate shook his head. "I'm sure he took off when he saw me coming up the road. You think it was the same man who was here earlier?"

"I don't know." She seemed confused, definitely upset. "You didn't see any sign of anyone?"

He shook his head, studying her. "What did he do?"

"He…he pushed me." She looked uncertain.

"He *pushed* you?" It dawned on him that she'd been half-afraid it had been him. That was why she'd reacted so oddly to him earlier.

"I know it sounds crazy, but someone *pushed* me. He knocked me down."

"But other than that, he didn't do anything to you?"

"No. He pushed me and then I guess he left." She shook her head as if realizing her story didn't make a lot of sense. Why would someone just push her and take off?

"All that matters is that you're okay."

She nodded. She wasn't okay. He could see that.

Apparently this had just been another message for him. "Well, it won't be a problem after tonight. I'll be here. But maybe you should consider staying at your family's ranch until I catch him."

She was shaking her head before he even finished talking. "I won't let him run me out of my own home."

An admirable attitude that he feared would get her killed. Except Roy Vaughn didn't have a score to settle with this woman. He was after Nate. Fooling with McKenna Bailey was just Roy Vaughn's way of letting Nate know he was in town—and was coming for him.

The problem was McKenna Bailey had inadvertently put herself right in the middle.

"If you're determined, then I'll just have to make sure no one bothers you," Nate said. "Were you working late?"

"No. I'd been over to the neighbors' and was headed back to the ranch when I remembered I'd left my paint samples in the house." She glanced toward the front yard. "I dropped them when—"

"I'll get them," he said. "I have a flashlight in my rig." He started for his truck when he heard her get out of hers. Turning, he watched her walk back toward the house, her own flashlight beam bobbing through the darkness as she moved.

He waited as she shone the light on the front of the house, then on the ground. He joined her even though he could see that she'd already found what she was looking for.

He walked her back to her truck. "Do you want me to follow you as far as your ranch?"

"No, it's not necessary. I'm fine now." As she climbed behind the wheel, he saw her hesitate. "I was afraid you'd changed your mind about staying out here."

He shook his head. "I'm sorry I was so late. I decided to have dinner in town. I thought you might still be here working, so I brought you something." He walked over to his pickup and came back with the foil-wrapped package. "It's just a piece of peach pie."

She peeked under the foil, seeming touched by his thoughtfulness, making him feel even more guilty. "Mmm, it smells wonderful. I think I forgot to eat today." She looked up at him. "Thank you."

"You're welcome."

"How did you know my favorite pie is peach?"

He smiled. "I guess I just got lucky. Well, see you in the morning."

"Wait, I forgot to give you a key to the house." She reached into the glove box for one of the extras she'd had made. "That will open the back door. This one's for the front. Be careful. That man might not have gone far."

"Don't worry." He took the keys, stepped away from her open window and, giving her a nod, walked to his truck.

Nate could feel her watching him all the way, as if she suspected he was the last man she should be trusting. Or it could have been his conscience that dogged him all the way back to his pickup— if he still had a conscience.

BEFORE GOING TO BED, Arlene Evans checked her e-mail hoping to see something more from Hank Monroe.

What she saw almost gave her heart failure. She hadn't completely forgotten about her young, handsome new client Jud Corbett. Originally she'd planned to pair him with her daughter Charlotte. That obviously wasn't happening right now given that Charlotte was almost eight months pregnant and not at her best.

So Arlene had set Jud up with a few local young women, feeling as though it was such a waste. A good-looking, eligible man like Jud. Jud's father, Grayson Corbett, had just bought a huge ranch down by the Missouri Breaks.

While Jud was the only one she'd seen so far, Arlene had heard there were four other brothers. She hoped they were as handsome and as eligible as Jud.

She was still hoping that her daughter Charlotte would come to her senses, give up the baby, get her shape back and hook up with Jud Corbett when she read the e-mail from Jud and let out a shriek.

She read it a second time, telling herself this had to be a bad dream. According to the e-mail, Jud had seen a woman on Arlene's rural Meet-A-Mate online service who he was very interested in meeting.

That was how the service worked, true enough.

But it was the name of the young woman whom Jud was requesting that sent Arlene into a tizzy.

Not only was the woman in question not a member of the online dating service, she wasn't even in town. And Arlene certainly wouldn't have put up the profile of her son Bo's former fiancée, Maddie Cavanaugh.

How had this happened? And now Jud was anxious to date the woman. Not only was Maddie Cavanaugh all wrong for him, Maddie was also Arlene's least favorite person in the world. She wasn't good enough for Jud Corbett!

Who had put Maddie's profile up on her Internet site? Arlene wanted to know. Was this supposed to be a joke? And how had Maddie's photo and information gotten up on the site without Arlene's permission? No one had that kind of access except for—

"Bo!" she bellowed as she stormed down the hallway to her son's room. *"Bo!"* She counted to ten before she threw open his door.

Storming in, she shut off his blaring stereo and glared at her son. He was lying sprawled on the bed, looking bored, as usual, and annoyed that she'd turned off his horrible music.

Bo was still handsome even though he had been letting himself go since his breakup with Maddie Cavanaugh. With him, Arlene still held out hope that he would meet the right woman and settle down.

"Did you put your former fiancée's profile and photo on my Internet dating service?" she demanded.

His smirk said it all.

"Why would you do such a thing knowing how I feel about Maddie Cavanaugh?"

"I thought you'd want to see her married off so she leaves me alone."

He had a point, although, as far as she knew, Maddie didn't want any more to do with Bo than he did with her. Maybe a whole lot less.

Arlene shook her head. If she didn't have a meeting with Hank Monroe, this little incident would have ruined her whole week.

"Leave my matchmaking business alone," she ordered. "Tomorrow I'll fix it so you won't be able to pull something like this again." Had she once hoped that she could interest her son in her business? That they could work together? What had she been thinking?

"Why don't you get out of this room and find yourself a nice young woman?" she snapped.

"What would I want with a nice young woman?" he asked with a leer.

She cuffed him on the side of the head.

"Hey, what was that about?" he whined, sounding hurt.

It was her lot in life, Arlene thought as she left his room, the loud music in her wake.

But she was determined not to let anything spoil her good mood. She was going to see Hank Monroe tonight. Not even her horrible children were going to spoil this.

She'd just e-mail Jud and tell him that Maddie Cavanaugh's profile was a mistake, that the girl didn't live here anymore, and then she'd find him someone else he could date until Charlotte came to her senses.

Still, it worried her. Jud had sounded way too interested in Maddie. Not that there was much chance Maddie would ever come back to Whitehorse for more than a visit.

But just in case, Arlene swore she would go to hell in a handbasket before she'd let Maddie Cavanaugh have Jud Corbett. She was saving him for Charlotte. One way or the other.

AFTER A NIGHT RIDDLED with bad dreams, McKenna awoke determined to put an end to her fears about the house—and Nate Dempsey.

She told herself she should be grateful that he

showed up when he did and it was time to stop second-guessing herself. But even as she thought it, she wondered if he'd spent the night digging up on the hillside behind the house—even though he said he hadn't the other time.

Skipping breakfast, since she'd eaten the peach pie Nate had brought her last night—and felt guilty the whole time for mistrusting his motives—she drove into Whitehorse to the sheriff's department.

Sheriff Carter Jackson would become her brother-in-law next month on the Fourth of July. Independence Day. McKenna had pointed that out to Eve, who'd only laughed.

"I like the idea of fireworks on our anniversary every year," Eve had said, getting that faraway look in her eyes.

McKenna had known Carter Jackson all her life, so she didn't feel strange showing up at his office with the paper she'd discovered under her floorboards. Carter would no doubt think she was overreacting for bringing it to him. But after a sleepless night worrying, she felt she had to show it to him.

"McKenna," he said, sounding happy to see her. But then, he'd been happy ever since Christmas when her sister had accepted his marriage proposal.

She gave him a hug, then took the chair he offered her.

"So what can I do for you?" he asked, leaning

back in his chair. "Tell me Eve didn't send you here with last-minute changes regarding the wedding."

"No, it's about the old Harper House."

"I heard you bought the place."

From his tone she could tell that her sister had shared her concerns with him. McKenna wished those concerns were unfounded. She opened her mouth to tell him about the man who'd pushed her last night, but in the light of day, she wasn't so sure anyone had pushed her. It made no sense. Why would the man hang around just to push her down and then take off? That was something a kid would do.

And, anyway, Nate would be staying on the property for a while. So the problem, if there even was one, was solved. And this way, word wouldn't somehow get back to her sister Eve. The last thing she needed was Eve worrying about her just weeks before big sis's wedding.

What concerned McKenna was what she'd found under the floorboards at the house. Even after twenty-one years, if there was any chance the people who'd worked there were in danger...

"I found something in the house that is...disturbing," she said as she removed the paper from her purse and carefully unrolled it to hand the sheet to him.

Carter frowned as he peered down at the blood-stained document. "What is this?"

"From what I can tell, it's a contract, a blood oath to take revenge against the people who hurt them."

"Where did you find this?"

"Under the floorboards in the house. I found out that it was once a home for troubled boys. Given the date of the Whitehorse Days event on the back, I can only assume those are the names of the boys who lived there twenty-one years ago."

"I heard rumors about the place when I was growing up," Carter said, studying the paper a moment before handing it back.

"So you don't think I should be concerned about it?" she asked him, knowing that was exactly what she wanted to hear.

He shook his head. "You know kids. At the time I'm sure they were angry and wanted to feel they had power over their lives. But, like you said, it's been twenty-one years. If they haven't acted on it by now…"

"They were too young to act on it back then, though. Now they'd be men in their late twenties to mid thirties," she said, wondering why she didn't just agree with him and leave it at that. "They would finally be old enough to make good on their threats." Not to mention consequences if not carried out.

"But why wait twenty-one years? They've been plenty old enough for years."

A question she'd asked herself. So why couldn't she just let it go? "I was wondering if you could find out what happened to these boys and the people who worked there."

He looked as if he thought that was a bad idea.

"I know it's an unusual request. But I would feel better if I knew for certain there was nothing to it."

Carter hesitated, then smiled. "Sure. Why not? If it will relieve your mind. I need you to keep your big sister sane. I'm worried she's going to get cold feet. You know Eve. She could just take off on horseback and we'd never see her again."

McKenna laughed. "Don't worry. She's not going anywhere. She loves you. She wouldn't miss that wedding for anything." At least McKenna hoped that was true.

Carter seemed to relax a little. "There is just one thing that would make her wedding day perfect," he said wistfully.

McKenna knew exactly what he was going to say. Her sister had looked nothing like either of their parents, Chester and Lila Bailey, or her sisters. From the time Eve was little she'd somehow known she was adopted even though their mother had denied it. As far as Lila Bailey had been concerned, Eve, McKenna and Faith were her children in every possible way—even if all three were adopted. Adopted through rather strange channels.

Eve had only recently discovered the truth about her adoption. While McKenna had no interest in her birth parents, Eve seemed unable to move on until she knew.

Unfortunately, since the adoptions hadn't exactly been legal, only one person apparently might know the truth about Eve's—and her brother Bridger Duvall's—birth mother. That person was Pearl Cavanaugh, who now lived in the nursing home following a stroke that had left her unable to speak.

"Knowing who her birth mother was and who she is would certainly make Eve happy," Carter said.

McKenna scoffed. "Eve *is* happy. And we all know who she is, and so does she. Knowing who her birth parents are won't change the woman Eve has become. How is Pearl doing, by the way?"

"Better. I understand she can say a few words. Bridger visits her every day. I think he's grown quite fond of her, and vice versa." Carter shook his head as if surprised by that since the two were definitely at cross purposes.

"What would happen if it all came out about the illegal adoptions?" McKenna asked. "The women responsible wouldn't have to go to prison, would they?"

"I certainly would hope not given that they're all up in years. But I doubt that would ever happen," he said. "I don't think Pearl is ever going to divulge any information about the babies—let alone the names of the others involved in the illegal adoption ring. Nina Mae Cross has Alzheimer's, so she would never stand trial."

"I hope Pearl takes it to her grave with her," McKenna said more adamantly than she'd intended. "I don't want to know. I figure my birth mother had her reasons for giving me up. If anything, I'm thankful."

Carter nodded. "I wish Eve felt that way."

A silence fell between them for a moment, then McKenna asked, "Would you mind making a copy of the paper I found? I'd like to keep it for now."

"No problem. I just don't want you taking it too seriously, all right?"

She nodded and waited while he went to make a copy.

"Off the top of my head, I know of at least two people who worked at Harper House," he said when he returned. "Rosemarie Blackmore and Frank Merkel. Both are still alive—so, see, there's nothing to what you found. But I'll look into what happened to the boys who lived there if it will make you feel better."

She took the document he handed her back, rolled it up and put it in her purse, relieved. "Thank you." She tried to settle down. She'd done everything she could. Now she would just wait until she heard from Carter.

There would be no point in her going by to talk to Rosemarie or Frank. What would she say anyway? That their lives might be in danger after twenty-one years? Crazy.

As crazy as worrying Carter—and ultimately her sisters—by telling the sheriff about last night.

If the sheriff thought there was any chance Frank and Rosemarie were in danger, he'd warn them. Why scare a couple of nice elderly people over nothing?

It *was* nothing. Just like that incident at the house last night. And now with Nate Dempsey staying out there, she had nothing to worry about but getting moved into her house.

AT THE NURSING HOME on the edge of Whitehorse, Pearl Cavanaugh looked up to see Bridger Duvall come into her room.

She closed her eyes as she listened to him pull up a chair next to her wheelchair.

"How are you today, Pearl?" he asked, just as he had every morning for months.

She opened her eyes with a sigh, pretending she wasn't glad to see him. While she used to dread his visits, she had to admit that she now looked forward to them and regretted the day when he would no longer come by.

That day would be when she told him the truth about his birth parents. His and Eve's, since the two were fraternal twins.

"It's a beautiful day out," he said. "Wouldn't you like to go outside?" He stood, waiting.

She gave a nod and he smiled down at her. "I thought you'd enjoy that." He went around behind her to push the wheelchair down the hall.

All of the nurses knew him and said hello, along with the doctors. Pearl liked hearing them compliment him on the restaurant he'd opened with her granddaughter, Laci. Northern Lights was doing well, from what she'd heard. That pleased her.

She hadn't been as pleased about Laci's engagement to Bridger. She'd originally worried about Bridger's motivations for getting close to her granddaughter. She'd prayed his reason wasn't the same one as why he'd come to Whitehorse and why he visited Pearl's nursing home every day.

Since then, though, she'd seen the two of them together. No two people had been so perfectly made for each other. Just the sight of them together made her smile. At least she thought she was smiling. Since the stroke, she couldn't be sure.

"We set a wedding date," Bridger said after circling the nursing home block and stopping to sneak her a flower from the ones growing in the beds out front.

She fingered the flower stem.

"We're getting married next Christmas," he said.

Her head came up, her eyes widening in surprise. She tried to form the words that were in her head, but nothing intelligible came out, to her growing frustration. At first not being able to speak had been a blessing in disguise. She couldn't have told Bridger what he wanted even if she was so inclined—or if he caught her in a weak moment.

But now she would give anything to get her speech back.

"Why such a long engagement?" he asked as if he could understand her gibberish.

She nodded weakly.

"Laci has her heart set on you being there." He knelt down in front of the wheelchair and took both her hands in his. "She wants you and her grandfather to be there to give her away. She has this dream that you'll be able to walk down the aisle with your husband Titus."

Tears welled in Pearl's eyes. She swallowed around the lump in her throat and squeezed his hand. She and Titus had raised her two grandchildren after their father was killed and their mother disappeared.

"Thank you." The words came out slowly, awkwardly, but he beamed at her progress.

"I am so glad you're getting better. I knew a stroke couldn't hold you down."

She looked into his dark eyes, worried that she wouldn't live long enough to see Laci married.

"I don't want you to get better just so one day you'll be able to tell me about my birth mother. You have to know that I have grown to care a great deal for you. It's Eve I'm worried about now. She's getting married next month. Carter wants a half dozen children at least," he said with a laugh. "I know why Eve isn't as sure about children."

Pearl nodded slowly. She *did* understand. For months she'd had nothing but time on her hands. Way too much time to think—and soul-search. She'd often wondered if she hadn't had the stroke, if she would have told Bridger and Eve what they wanted to know. She'd always sworn she would take what she knew about the Whitehorse Sewing Circle's more secret activities to her grave.

She and the others had placed so many babies

over the years. She knew what they had done was illegal in the eyes of the law, but she didn't believe in laws that made it difficult for those who wanted children not to be able to have them, no matter their age, their income, their abilities. Love for the child was the only criterion she could see. She would still stand behind everything she had done—even if it meant going to prison.

She'd always believed it was best if the adopted children didn't know about their birth parents. The stroke and getting to know Bridger Duvall had changed everything, she realized. She now knew the frustration of being unable to have something she desperately wanted or needed.

She also knew that she wouldn't have kept records of the information about each baby's birth parents unless she'd thought she might need it one day.

That day was near. She was able to say more words and had been practicing writing. Soon she would be able to tell Bridger what he wanted— and thus tell Eve Bailey, as well.

Eve's wedding was next month. Bridger had already informed her that he would come by to pick her up so she didn't have to miss it since he and Laci were catering the affair and he also didn't want her to miss the food.

Pearl knew what Bridger wanted for Eve's

wedding day. It was why she'd been doing so much soul-searching lately. She'd seen how haunted both Bridger and Eve had been by their need to know who they were. She thanked God she hadn't died, the information dying with her. She alone knew the codes to the birth parents.

She'd done that to protect the others in the Whitehorse Sewing Circle.

And now she questioned whether she had the right to keep such a secret. But what would the truth do to those involved? Bring them the peace they so desperately sought? Or, in some cases, destroy their lives?

Chapter Ten

As McKenna came out of the sheriff's department, she was surprised to see Flynn Garrett driving by. He slowed to a stop in the middle of the street and rolled down his window.

"Hello," he said, sounding genuinely glad to see her. "I had a great time the other night."

"Me, too."

He seemed to study her for a long moment. "Home ownership seems to agree with you."

She smiled and nodded, although that wasn't the case.

He glanced toward the sheriff's department. "Is everything all right?"

She knew he'd seen her coming out of the office and must wonder why. "My future brother-in-law is the sheriff."

"That's good," he said. "But why do I get the feeling there's more? You looked like you'd lost your best friend when you came out of there."

Tears blurred her eyes. She bit her lip and glanced away.

"Hey," he said. "Whatever it is, you can tell me."

She nodded and swallowed. This was so unlike her. She'd been through so much lately. Her emotions were right on the edge.

"Is there someplace you have to be?" she asked. "I could use a cup of coffee."

"You got it," he said. "Hop in."

He took her to the only coffee shop in town. It was empty this late in the morning in a town like Whitehorse. He ordered them two black coffees and they sat at a table by the window.

"Okay, tell me what's going on," he said, not touching his coffee.

"Promise you won't think I'm crazy?"

He laughed. "Too late for that. I already think you're crazy for buying that house."

She told him about the man who'd come by supposedly looking for work and about being pushed down last night.

Flynn looked skeptical. "So you think this man hung around to push you off your porch?"

"See, I told you it sounds crazy."

"Did you get a look at him?"

She shook her head.

"Pretty odd. Unless, of course, it was a ghost."

"I don't believe in ghosts—and, believe me,

the hand I felt on my back was no ghost's. That's not all." She opened her shoulder bag, took out the piece of rolled-up paper and handed it to him, desperately seeking another opinion.

His eyes widened as he unrolled it.

"Apparently it's a kind of contract. I found it under a floorboard in the house. I'm pretty sure the names on it belong to the boys who lived there when it was a home for troubled youth."

He let out a low whistle. "So what do you make of it?" he asked as he handed the paper back.

"That's just it. I don't know."

"What did your future brother-in-law say when you showed it to him?"

As she put the paper back in her shoulder bag, she glanced up at him, only a little surprised he'd figured out why she'd gone to Carter. "You think I was wrong to show it to him?"

"Not at all. Quite frankly it gives me the creeps."

She let out a relieved sigh. "I can't tell you how glad I am that someone else feels that way. It really upset me when I found it." She cupped her coffee mug in her hands and stared down into the dark brew as she breathed in the rich scent, more calm than she'd been in days.

"Your future brother-in-law wasn't worried about it?"

She shook her head. "It *has* been twenty-one

years. If the boys were going to do something, wouldn't they have done it?"

Flynn shrugged. "Makes sense, I guess."

"The sheriff is going to see if any of the people who worked at Harper House—"

"Got whacked?"

She grimaced at his frankness. "There are several people who were employed there who are still alive and living here in Whitehorse, so I'm sure there is nothing to it. Just hurt and angry kids finding a little power in the idea of retribution, just like Carter said."

"Yeah. You did the right thing showing it to the sheriff, though."

Just as she'd done the right thing telling Flynn Garrett about it, she thought as she felt a sense of relief. He was easy to talk to and didn't confuse her the way Nate Dempsey did. With Flynn, she knew exactly what he wanted from her. Typical male.

But Nate Dempsey? She didn't even think he was attracted to her. He'd certainly never acted as if he was. And he *had* stood her up for their date. Nor had he bothered to ask her out again.

"So what are you doing tonight?" Flynn asked, making her realize she'd been lost in thought. About Nate. "I could go for another one of those steaks at that restaurant. What do you say?"

She had to laugh. Here she was thinking about

Nate when a very handsome cowboy was asking her to dinner. "Yes, but I have to get out to the house and get some painting done first. I'm running late as it is."

"No problem. I could pick you up out there if that would save you time."

Why not? She could bathe at the house since the upstairs bath had running water. She would be glad when the shower was fixed downstairs. All she had to do was pick up a change of clothes at the ranch.

"That would be great," she said, wondering if she'd agreed to having Flynn pick her up at the house because she wanted Nate Dempsey to see that other men were interested in dating her.

Sick, she thought. She'd never thrown herself at any man and she certainly wasn't going to start now. Nor was she going to use Flynn to try to make Nate jealous.

"You know, it would be easier for you if I just met you at the restaurant like last time."

"Not a chance. I'll pick you up at the house. It's not a problem. Really. This time it's a real date," he said with a meaningful look.

She smiled, wondering about the look—and him being so agreeable to picking her up at the house he'd lost in the bidding auction.

Flynn Garrett was the type of man who might think buying a woman two steaks and a bottle of champagne warranted staying over at her house after a "real" date.

He was going to be disappointed if that was the case.

SHERIFF CARTER JACKSON hadn't wanted to worry McKenna. He was sure there was nothing to the paper she'd found under her floorboards at the house.

Yet at the same time it was the kind of thing that wasn't easily brushed off as of no consequence.

He made a few calls to people he thought might have known someone who worked out at Harper House during the time the boys had been incarcerated there.

The fact that Frank Merkel and Rosemarie Blackmore were still alive pretty much proved that the boys hadn't followed through with their threat.

Finding the boys proved harder. Some had apparently been adopted and thus had different surnames. Others just appeared to have dropped off the radar. He suspected some had died; some might have gone to prison.

He hadn't found anyone else he knew who'd worked at Harper House, either, when he looked up to see his fiancée in his office doorway. It never failed. Every time he saw Eve Bailey she took his breath away. He couldn't believe the woman had agreed to marry him. Falling in love with her was the only smart thing he'd ever done.

"Hey," he said, unable to hold back a grin. "What a surprise."

"Are you busy? If I'm interrupting something important—"

"Are you kidding? Nothing is more important than you," he said, coming around his desk to give her a kiss. He motioned to a chair and took one opposite her. "What's up?"

He just assumed it would be something about the wedding since it was only a few weeks away now.

"I have a favor to ask," Eve said.

Eve Bailey wasn't the kind of woman who asked for help if she could prevent it.

"It's about my sister."

He knew which sister at once. Eve had been concerned about McKenna buying the old Harper place. Carter doubted McKenna had shown her sister what she'd found in the house, which was just as well since he knew it would only upset Eve and he was trying desperately to keep that from happening in the days before the wedding.

"Faith?" he asked, even though he knew better.

"No, McKenna." Eve took a breath and let it out slowly. "I know you think I shouldn't be worried about her and that house. But now there is a man who is hanging around out there. When

I was at the house yesterday I could tell that McKenna was upset about something. That man was there."

Carter frowned. "Someone I know?"

She shook her head. "He was driving a black pickup with Dempsey Construction on the side. She said his name was Nate."

He nodded. "You want me to see what I can find out about him?"

"Would you mind?" She sounded so relieved he couldn't help but lean across the space between them and kiss her.

"Not to worry. I'll get right on it. If there is something amiss, I'll take care of it."

Eve blessed him with a smile and he walked her to the door. He'd promised himself and her that they wouldn't make love until they were married, but it was getting more difficult with each passing day.

"I can't wait to be your wife," she whispered as she brushed against him.

He groaned. "You're a vixen," he whispered.

She laughed. "You're the one who said we had to wait."

"Yeah."

"You could change your mind."

He shook his head. "No, I want to do this right. We have the rest of our lives as husband and wife—and, believe you me, I intend to make up for lost time."

She laughed and kissed him. "I can hardly wait. You won't forget about checking on this Nate Dempsey guy. I took down his plate number, if that helps." She handed him a slip of paper with a license plate from Park County.

Carter studied his bride-to-be with admiration and a little concern. "You're really worried about this guy."

She nodded. "It's just a feeling."

"Then I'll see what I can find out right away."

McKENNA HAD PLANNED to pick up paint and supplies and head for the house. The last place she'd intended to go was Frank Merkel's on the edge of town.

But after showing Flynn Garrett the document she'd found, she felt even more worried. Flynn had taken it seriously, although she suspected the sheriff had played down his concern.

A small dust devil whirled through the yard as she parked and sat for a moment trying to talk herself out of this. What was she going to say, anyway?

She saw the curtain in the front room move and decided since she'd driven out this far…

Climbing out of the truck, she heard a dog bark in the backyard, then a deep male voice yell at the canine to shut up.

Before she even reached the front door, it

swung open and a large, dark-haired and bearded man filled the doorway. He wore faded overalls and a flannel shirt with holes in the elbows, and his feet were bare.

"Frank Merkel?" McKenna said, questioning the impulse to come out here.

"Yeah?" He had a broad, flat face that looked as if it had been slammed in a door and flat, dark eyes that stared blankly at her.

This had seemed like a good idea a few minutes and miles ago. "I'm McKenna Bailey."

His eyes narrowed.

He looked past her to her pickup, then shifted his gaze back to her face. "What do you want?" His tone was even less friendly than his expression.

"I just bought the old Harper House—"

"You have the wrong person." He started to close the door.

"Wait. I heard you used to work there. I wanted to warn you."

"Warn me?" he demanded through the crack between door and jamb.

All she could see now was one of his eyes. "I found something in the house, a piece of paper that the boys wrote on. I think you might be in danger."

Her words echoed off the closed door as he slammed it. In the backyard, the dog began to bark again.

She didn't have the wrong person. She'd seen his change of expression when she'd mentioned Harper House. She stood for a moment, thinking he might come back. Then, admitting this had been a mistake, she walked back through the patch of weeds to her pickup.

Angry with Frank Merkel for dismissing her concerns so rudely and furious with herself for thinking talking to him was a good idea in the first place, she started the engine and checked her watch. She needed to get out to the house. Her sisters would be there soon to help paint. She needed the help, and they would both be understandably angry if she wasn't there when they arrived.

But she had one more stop to make and then she would put this whole blood-oath thing behind her.

As McKenna pulled up in the driveway of the small clapboard house at the end of the Whitehorse street, she saw a small white-haired woman out watering her flower beds.

The woman looked up as McKenna got out of her truck and walked up the narrow sidewalk. The street was quiet except for the groan of a lawn mower a block away and the coo of a dove on a telephone wire overhead.

That was something McKenna had missed living in a larger city: the sound of birds instead of traffic. In Whitehorse, if four cars went by, you could bet something was going on.

Rosemarie Blackmore gave her the once-over and returned to watering her flowers. Ever since McKenna had purchased the old Harper House she'd felt as if people were treating her strangely. She suspected Rosemarie knew why she was here and wanted none of it—much like Frank Merkel.

But, damn it all, she had to try. She'd never forgive herself if something happened to them and she hadn't even tried to warn them. As the new owner of Harper House, she felt responsible.

"Mrs. Blackmore?"

Rosemarie flicked a look at her but said nothing.

"I need to talk to you about Harper House," McKenna said, getting right to the heart of it. "If you could just spare me a minute. It's important."

Rosemarie made a displeased face, but she shut off the water, wiped her hands on the apron she was wearing and said, "Well, come on in, then."

McKenna followed her inside. Rosemarie Blackmore looked like a grandmother, from the countless knickknacks everywhere to the crocheted doilies and the knitting bag beside her chair with a half-finished afghan spilling out of it. Across from it was a worn leather chair with a stack of hunting magazines next to it—no doubt just as it had been when her husband was alive.

"I'm McKenna Bailey," she said once they

were standing in the cluttered living room. "I just bought the old Harper House."

"I know who you are," the older woman said impatiently.

"I understand you used to work at what was known as Harper House when it was a home for troubled boys."

"It's no *secret*. I used to cook out there." A large yellow tomcat came strutting into the room. He wound his way around Rosemarie's legs and purred loudly. As the elderly woman stooped to pick up the cat, she motioned McKenna into a chair, then took one herself, the large cat on her lap as she waited for the next question with impatient politeness.

"When did you work there?"

Rosemarie shrugged. "A few months in the early eighties, I believe. Why do you care about this anyway?"

"I heard that some of the boys might have been mistreated."

She snorted. "So you're one of those people who thinks they should have been pampered. Let me tell you something—those boys were hellions. I lived in fear every minute I was in that house."

"I had no idea they were that bad," McKenna said.

"Bad? They were evil. The whole lot of them were destined to become hardened criminals."

"But they were so *young*," McKenna said.

Rosemarie snorted again. "Their characters were already forged by the time they ended up at Harper House." She hugged the cat closer as if chilled.

"Can you tell me who else worked there?"

"Why?" she asked suspiciously.

"I'm trying to find one of the boys," McKenna said.

"I can't imagine why."

"Would you know any of them or how to contact them?"

She shoved the cat off her lap. He skulked away, meowing loudly. "No, I wouldn't." She rose to her feet. "I stayed in the kitchen, did my job, then got the devil out of there. They were a rowdy bunch of boys. It wasn't my place to say how they should be raised. They were boys nobody wanted and there was a reason for it."

"But you *did* hear things."

"I didn't hear anything. I didn't see anything."

"You never heard from any of them?"

Rosemarie's eyes widened. "Why would I?"

"I just thought there might have been one who appreciated your cooking, one you might have gotten close to." McKenna knew she was clutching at straws, but she couldn't help thinking of the boy she'd seen in the third-floor window that day so many years ago.

Clearly agitated, Rosemarie shook her head. "I didn't want to see any of them ever again and I hope I don't. They were like wild dogs. I saw the way they looked at me each day when I left." She cringed. "Now, if you'll excuse me, I have things to do. Leo will be wanting his lunch."

It wasn't near lunchtime, and her husband, Leo, had been dead for four years. But McKenna didn't argue. She rose, thanking Rosemarie for her time.

"There is one other thing," McKenna said, unable to leave without at least warning the woman. "I found something in the house. A note the boys wrote," she said, playing it down. "They sounded angry and made some threats...."

Rosemarie was visibly agitated now. "You really should go."

"I just thought you should be warned. I doubt there is anything to worry about, but if any of them should come by—"

"I don't see why you want that house," Rosemarie said. "Makes no sense."

Makes no sense to anyone in this town, McKenna thought. And lately it hadn't been making a lot of sense to her either.

"Please, just take care of yourself," McKenna said as she left, Rosemarie closing the door firmly behind her.

McKenna was mentally kicking herself for upsetting Rosemarie as she started to climb into her truck when Nate Dempsey pulled up.

"Hey," he said as if surprised to see her. "I thought you'd be painting like crazy by now."

Why did she get the feeling he'd been looking for her? "I should be. I decided to talk to a couple of people who used to work at Harper House."

"Why?" he asked, sounding worried.

"I want to know more about the place."

"Do you think that's a good idea? You might not like what you find out. Unless you've already found out something that has you upset."

Did he know about the paper she'd found? But then, how could he? And why hadn't she shown it to him? After all, he was staying out at the place. If she trusted him…

"I'm headed for the house now. My sisters are coming over to help me paint."

He nodded. "I came in to pick up a couple of plumbing parts. By the time you get to the house I'll have your shower working for you."

"Thank you. Let me know what I owe you for parts…."

He waved that off as he drove away, leaving her standing in the street. She couldn't help but feel that he was upset with her. She reminded herself that he thought she was crazy for buying

Harper House. No wonder he thought she was wrong to go around digging up its past.

As she turned toward her pickup, she glanced back at Rosemarie Blackmore's small white house.

The tiny gray-haired woman was standing in the front window. She was staring after Nate Dempsey.

McKenna saw the expression on the woman's face and felt her knees go weak.

Rosemarie Blackmore looked as if she'd seen a ghost.

Chapter Eleven

Her sisters were waiting for her when McKenna reached the house. She noticed that Nate's pickup was nowhere to be seen—just Eve's parked out front.

"Sorry. I got hung up," she said as she quickly began to unload the paint she'd purchased and the supplies.

"We just got here," Faith said, even though Eve was giving McKenna a questioning eye.

"Nate was leaving as we came in," Eve said.

"I guess he got my shower fixed, then," she said as she headed into the house with a gallon of paint dangling from each hand. "I'm going to have to quit early. I have a date with Flynn tonight."

"Flynn?" Eve and Faith echoed behind her, making her smile.

"He's the one I had dinner with Saturday night after the auction. We're having dinner again tonight." She grinned at them as she stopped to open the door.

"Flynn?" she heard Eve say again behind her. "How many men is she seeing?"

Faith giggled. "She's just having fun."

"Fun? You call this fun?" Eve said as she and Faith followed McKenna into the house.

They painted throughout the rest of the morning. Eve had brought a picnic basket. They ate sandwiches on the porch and discussed how the work was going. Well, since all of the rooms upstairs were painted except for the trim, and they would have that done by midafternoon and quit for the day so McKenna could get ready for her date.

"So tell us about Flynn," Eve said.

McKenna smiled over at her sister. "You worry too much."

"Right."

"He's picking me up here, so if you're that curious, you can stay and meet him," McKenna said.

"So you aren't serious about him if you'd let us meet him," Eve said and took a bite of her sandwich.

"I'm not serious about anyone," McKenna protested. "I'm going to be too busy getting my business going to worry about a man."

Eve nodded, her gaze saying she didn't believe

it for a minute. "So tell me about this Nate who's helping with your house."

McKenna shrugged. "There isn't much to tell. He needed a place to board his horse, so we traded services."

"He sure didn't stick around long once he saw us," Eve commented.

"I'm sure he had things to do," McKenna said, wondering where he'd gone—and why he did seem to make himself scarce when her sisters were around.

NATE DROVE HIS PICKUP down the dusty, rough road, keeping his eyes peeled on his rearview mirror for any sign of another vehicle.

He was certain he hadn't been followed, but for days he'd felt as if he was being watched. It surprised him that Roy Vaughn hadn't made his move. But, then again, Vaughn had always loved playing cat and mouse—just as long as he got to be the cat.

Nate couldn't be sure that the man who called himself Hal Turner was indeed Roy Vaughn. But Vaughn had been a big kid, a bully, and he'd liked to think of himself as the next legendary Hal Turner.

That was why for years Nate had found himself looking over his shoulder, expecting at any moment to feel the burning prick of a knife blade in his back. He remembered only too well the switchblade that Roy Vaughn had kept under his mattress. It took a dark soul to like killing up close and personal with a blade.

So what was Vaughn waiting for? That's what bothered Nate as he drove. That and the fact that he hadn't seen Lucky.

"I'm not afraid of Roy," Lucky had said.

"You should be."

Lucky had only shrugged. "Maybe I'm enough like him that he's always left me alone."

Lucky had always liked to think himself tougher than he was. But, thinking back, for some reason Roy Vaughn *had* left Lucky alone. Maybe it was because Vaughn had had Nate and Johnny to pick on.

The road wound through a narrow canyon in the Bear Paw Mountains. Pine trees grew lush green against towering vertical slabs of sandstone. Not far up the road, the canyon opened some to end in a jumble of rock. A box canyon. A dead end.

Nate slowed the pickup, on alert. He'd seen the tracks in the road where someone had been up here right after the rain. But that could have been anyone. He'd seen no sign of another living soul. Not unusual in this part of the country. Montana had an average population of six-point-two people per square mile—except up here, where it was more like zero-point-three people.

In this part of the state there were more cows than people. Hell, cows outnumbered people in Montana three to one.

Nate stopped the pickup at the end of the road and sat for a moment, window down, just listening. This is where they'd found Roy Vaughn the one and only time he'd escaped from Harper House. Nate would never forget the look on Vaughn's face. He'd been holed up in some rocks at the back of the canyon. The fool hadn't realized it was a box canyon—no way out.

Mostly Vaughn hadn't realized that Harper House was the same way. No way out back then. Except maybe death.

Nate always wondered if Vaughn hadn't wished for that very thing when he saw the Harper House's old Suburban drive up and knew he was trapped. Worse than trapped. Caught.

Shoving away the memory, Nate cautiously got out. The ground had dried since the rain. Heat beat down from a sun positioned overhead. The ponderosa pines glistened, a silky green. There was no breath of air down in here. No sound. The stillness would get to anyone, Nate told himself as he pulled his weapon from his holster and walked toward the back of the canyon wall. To the place where they'd found Vaughn hunkered down.

He'd looked like a wild animal. His eyes

glowing in the blare of the flashlight beam. Everyone had known he would head for the mountains if he ever got away. He missed the mountains the most, he used to say.

It had taken four of them to restrain Vaughn. He'd fought like the animal he appeared to be. But that wasn't what haunted Nate to this day. It was the sound Vaughn had made. A high-pitched keening sound. The sound Nate suspected someone made when they were being tortured—right before they were killed.

As he neared the rocks, he felt his pulse quicken. His senses intensified; he thought he could feel Vaughn's presence here. He peered into the shadows of the rocks, the gun in his hand, the hair standing up on the back of his neck.

He'd thought just by coming back to Harper House he would have drawn Vaughn out by now. Instead Roy Vaughn was toying with him. Or maybe he was waiting to see if Nate found Johnny's body, all the time knowing that wasn't going to happen because he'd moved it.

Either way, Nate knew he'd been a fool to think that Vaughn would make it easy for him.

But he also couldn't keep looking over his shoulder for the rest of his life. Vaughn was in town. Nate was convinced he was the man McKenna had seen. It would end where it had started. But apparently on Vaughn's terms.

Or maybe it would end in this canyon, right here, right now. Vaughn would know that Nate would search him out. Hell, he could be watching Nate from some of the rocks higher up the canyon wall and laughing his ass off that Nate had been so stupid as to come here alone.

Even armed, Nate knew he would be no match for the Roy Vaughn he'd known. The kid had been a bull, strong and tough. Nate hated to imagine what he was like as a grown man with years of cruelty behind him.

But unfortunately—or maybe fortunately—Vaughn wasn't hiding in the canyon. At least not today.

Which meant he could be anywhere. Even at Harper House.

MCKENNA DIDN'T SEE Nate all afternoon. After lunch, some of their friends came by, including the sheriff and a couple of deputies.

She saw Eve and the sheriff, their heads together, discussing something that looked serious. But a few moments later she saw Eve give Carter a kiss and tried to relax. This wedding had to go off as planned. McKenna was the maid of honor and felt responsible for seeing that nothing went wrong.

At one point the sheriff pulled McKenna aside. "I did some checking on people who used to work out here." He seemed to hesitate. "Quite a few them *are* deceased, but the only ones with foul play indicated were the Cherrys."

McKenna nodded. She'd grown up on the edge of Old Town Whitehorse, so she knew the story of Norman and Alma Cherry only too well. Norman had allegedly taken his wife down to the root cellar in the middle of the night, put a bullet in her head, then one in his own. No one had ever known why.

"Is it possible they were the first?" McKenna asked.

Carter shook his head. "That was more than thirty years ago. The paper you found was dated only twenty-one years ago."

She had a terrible thought. "Unless this death pact wasn't something new to Harper House. The Winthrops told me it's been operating over thirty years. Maybe these boys got the idea from others who had lived there before them."

"Let's not jump to conclusions," he said. "I'm still doing some checking."

"Who else is deceased?"

Carter handed her a list of the names.

She scanned it and froze. "Hal Turner?"

"Killed in a hunting accident."

McKenna fought to breathe. "A man stopped by here the other day. He said his name was Hal Turner."

"Obviously not the same Hal Turner," Carter said and then seemed to notice how shaken she was. "Am I missing something here?"

"What if the man I saw was one of the boys using the name of someone who used to work there?"

"McKenna, you're starting to worry me now. I think you're letting this get to you. Hal Turner didn't work there. He was one of the first guys who lived there." He took the list from her. "All of these deaths were ruled an accident, okay?"

She nodded numbly. It was too much of a coincidence that the man had used that name. She'd known he was lying at the time. Now she knew Hal Turner had been one of the boys who'd lived in the house. "What about the names on the list that I found?"

"Three of them are deceased," Carter said. "Lyle Weston, Steven Cross and Andrew Charles. Bobby French is serving time in prison in Oregon. The others I haven't been able to find. But, as I told you, some of them were adopted, so their names would have been changed when they were still juveniles."

She nodded. That left only three names on the list: Roy Vaughn, Lucky Thomas and Denny Jones. She felt some relief that the others were accounted for.

"By the way, I see you have someone staying out back," the sheriff said.

She cringed. So like Carter to have noticed even though Nate's tent wasn't visible from the house. The only way Carter could have noticed was if he had looked around the property.

"Nate Dempsey," she said, trying to sound as casual as possible. "He's trading work for boarding his horse. I told him he could camp out there to make it easier for him to work on the house."

"What do you know about him?" Carter asked.

"He fixed my shower and made some other repairs that will make it possible for me to move in soon," she said maybe a little too cheerfully.

"How long is he staying?"

Good question. "Just until I move into the house," she said, thinking that was probably true. As much as he apparently liked his solitude, she couldn't see him hanging around after that. Unless he was the one who'd been digging in her yard—and hadn't found what he was looking for.

She expected Carter to interrogate her further and was surprised when he didn't.

By late afternoon the painting was done. Tomorrow, if it didn't rain, the furniture would be brought in.

She'd painted her office a sunny yellow. The bedroom she'd painted a pale lilac like the trees just outside her window. The other rooms were varying shades of warm, rich color.

"Too girlie," one of the off-duty deputies said about the color she'd chosen for her bedroom. "Didn't they have a nice tan?" he only half joked.

"White's good, too," said Deputy Nicolas Giovanni.

"A little colorphobic, are you, Nicolas?" Eve teased. "Are you trying to tell me that Laney is painting all the walls in your new house white?"

"I suggested it," Nicolas said with a grin.

"And he lived to tell about it," Carter added. "We've got to go. You have everything under control out here?"

McKenna nodded and thanked them all. After the men left, she noticed that Nate's pickup was still gone. What did he do when he wasn't here? She had no idea. He'd said he had business in Whitehorse. None of her business.

The men all left promising to help with the furniture move. After they'd gone, Eve said she had to go, as well.

"What? You aren't going to stay and meet Flynn?" McKenna asked.

"No reason to," Eve said. "You aren't serious about him."

"Well, I'd like to meet him if he's as handsome as she says," Faith joked.

As McKenna watched her sisters leave, she thought how she'd never been able to fool Eve even when they were young. Eve knew her too well.

SHERIFF CARTER JACKSON had just walked into his house when he got the call.

"You were asking about people who used to work out there at the old Harper place?"

"Yes." He recognized the woman's voice as that of Mabel Brooks, an eighty-something ranch woman who raised sheep on her place outside of town. He didn't bother to question how she'd heard he'd been asking around.

"I remember the first couple who worked out there," Mabel was saying. "Cherry was their name. Both dead. Then there was Lloyd Frasier. Also dead."

Carter listened, jotting down the new names going back to when Harper House had begun taking in troubled boys. All of the former workers were deceased. Heart attacks, car wrecks, ranch and hunting accidents. Except for the Cherrys' murder/suicide.

The longer he listened, the more concerned he became. A lot of bad luck had befallen anyone who'd worked at the place, apparently.

Still, he thought as he hung up, Frank Merkel and Rosemarie Blackmore were fine. Could it be a coincidence so many of the people had died? Could be their ages, he reminded himself. The place had sprung up more than thirty years before. The youngest of people who worked there had to be over fifty now, many much older than that.

He realized he hadn't heard back on his request for information on Nate Dempsey, and now that he knew the man was staying on McKenna's property…

He called, this time ringing the chief of police in Paradise at home. The joke about small-town sheriffs and chiefs of police was that more people knew their home phone number than that of their office.

"You're inquiring about Nate Dempsey?" the chief asked, sounding amused. "May I ask why?"

"With all the construction fraud nowadays, I was just checking to make sure there wasn't a problem with him working on a house up here."

"He picked up a hammer again? He must be doing some moonlighting on his vacation, then," the chief said.

Huh? "Are you saying he isn't employed in construction? He's driving a truck with Dempsey Construction on the side."

"He *was* in the construction business with his brother. That must be his brother's pickup he's driving. But Nate hasn't worked construction for almost ten years now."

Chapter Twelve

After everyone was gone, McKenna felt restless. She finally walked up the creek to where Nate Dempsey had pitched his tent. She saw his Appaloosa on the other side of the fence, grazing in the summer sun, but no sign of Nate. His horse trailer was parked next to the barn, his pickup gone.

Blue came over to the fence to give her a nuzzle. She rubbed the horse's neck and thought about peeking into Nate's tent. *For what?* she asked herself. *What is it you need to know before you trust the man?*

At the sound of a vehicle coming up the road she turned to see a black pickup headed this way. The last thing she wanted to do was get caught out here by his tent, but it was too late to escape unnoticed.

Nate drove up the drive past the house to park next to the barn.

She could only watch him as he got out and strode toward her. It wasn't until he was almost to her that she could see his face in the shadow of his Western straw hat brim. He didn't look happy.

"That horse can be temperamental," he snapped.

"Yeah, I can see that," she said, giving Blue one last pat before she moved away from the fence. "He seems to be settled in fine. What about you?"

"As you can see, I have everything I need."

Apparently.

"How did the painting go?" he asked as if trying to make conversation, although clearly something else was on his mind. "I thought your sisters would still be here with you."

"They just left. We got the upstairs done. They're coming back tomorrow with a load of my furniture."

"You're going to move in before you finish all the painting?" He sounded more than surprised.

"It will make it easier to get the work done if I'm staying here. We plugged in the old fridge in the kitchen. It works. So I'll bring some food out. My new stove should be delivered soon. I'll be fine."

He nodded but didn't look happy about it.

"And you'll be here if there's any trouble, right?"

She hated the fear that seemed to close her throat at the thought that he'd hightail it the moment she moved in.

"I'll be here," he said, not sounding in the least happy about that, either.

"Great." She wanted to ask him what he was really doing here. Not for a place to board his horse. He'd said he was here on business. He just hadn't mentioned for how long.

She glanced at her watch, telling herself that once she was settled in the house maybe it would be best if he left. She would always wonder what it was that he really wanted. He still hadn't asked her out, although she'd expected him to mention Whitehorse Days again. He hadn't, though.

"Well, I need to get ready for my…" She bit her tongue, but it was too late. "Date." She groaned inwardly. Why had she mentioned her date? Was she expecting some kind of reaction from him? Say, something akin to jealousy? Well, if she was, she was sadly disappointed.

He said nothing as she took a couple steps backward. She turned and walked toward the house as quickly as she could, mentally kicking herself the entire way.

FLYNN GARRETT WAS nothing if not prompt. As he climbed out of his truck, she saw him glance up at the house and shake his head.

"Want to see what we've done upstairs?" she asked.

"A waste of paint," he said but smiled as he did. "Maybe some other time. I have us a reservation for seven and we'll be late if we don't leave now. Rain check on the tour?"

"Sure." Although she was disappointed. But she understood on some level that he didn't want to see the house he'd tried to buy himself.

They ordered steaks again. No champagne this time. Conversation seemed harder this time, and McKenna wondered if she'd made a mistake by having Flynn pick her up at the house. He'd been overly quiet ever since, as if brooding.

"I did something crazy today," she said.

He looked up expectantly from his dessert.

"I went by the homes of the two people who used to work at Harper House and warned them they might be in danger."

He put down his fork. "You're kidding? I thought the sheriff told you there was nothing to worry about."

"Yes, but I felt I had to."

"And?"

"Neither appreciated my concern. Both pretty much threw me out."

"Ingrates," he said. "You do realize that you may have just put yourself in jeopardy, though, don't you? I mean, if you're right and these guys are coming back after twenty-one years, seeking vengeance, they probably wouldn't appreciate you butting in."

She hadn't thought of that. "More than likely all I did was scare a couple of old people for no reason. I'm beginning to think that I'm dead wrong about this."

"Interesting turn of phrase." He smiled. It was nothing like Nate's smile. "I wouldn't worry about it. If you're right, by buying Harper House you've already put yourself in jeopardy. You probably didn't make it any worse today."

"Thanks," she said with a laugh. "I knew you'd make me feel better."

"Sorry." He frowned. "I just wish I'd known you were considering doing that. I would have tried to talk you out of it."

She nodded, knowing he wouldn't have been able to, but no reason to tell him how stubborn she could be. "Fortunately, I don't think there is anything to it. After all these years, what are the chances?"

"Well, you gave it your best shot," he said.

Yes, hadn't she? She frowned as she remembered Rosemarie's expression as she'd watched Nate drive away. No doubt it was from being frightened by the news McKenna had brought her. Or maybe she'd mistakenly thought Nate was one of the boys, grown now.

She reminded herself again that his name hadn't been on the list. That she and Rosemarie Blackmore were both a little crazy.

"I have to tell you," Flynn said, drawing her attention back to their date. "When I picked you up at the house this evening I was thinking about what you found there. The paper. Quite frankly, I'm not sure you're safe there. Maybe you should stay at your family's ranch until you're sure there's nothing to all this."

She thought about mentioning the man she had living on the creek behind the house but thought better of it. The fewer people who knew about her arrangement, the better.

"Maybe," she agreed, then changed the subject, and in a few minutes Flynn was telling her funny stories about the ranches he'd worked on, his worries about her apparently forgotten.

IT WAS DARK BY THE time Flynn dropped her off at the house. He left the engine running.

"I have an early day tomorrow," he said as he got out and walked her to the door.

This time when he kissed her McKenna knew it was their last date—and she realized she was fine with that.

She watched him drive away, wondering if Nate was camped on the creek. Or if he'd gone into town. Or maybe even left. And told herself the only reason she cared was that she wanted him around for a while. Just until she got completely moved in. Until she was sure the strange man wouldn't be back. Or that there really was nothing to the contract she'd found under the floorboards.

But the truth was she wanted him around. She had no idea what it was about him that drew her to him. These feelings made no sense, especially since he obviously didn't share them.

She pulled her pickup keys from her shoulder bag. There was really no reason to go into the house since she was still staying down at her family's ranch until her furniture was moved in tomorrow.

But she was here and the night was young. She might as well take a look at the upstairs, admire the work they'd done and think about where she'd put the furniture when it arrived.

Unlocking the door, she reached in and turned on a light before stepping inside. The wood floors gleamed. She couldn't wait to finish the painting. The house already had a different feel to it, didn't it?

She glanced through to the kitchen and the window that looked out on the backyard—and the creek. She could see a flickering light through the branches on the cottonwoods along the creek. A campfire. Nate. Her pulse took off, heart beating a little faster. He was here.

Climbing the steps to the top floor, she turned on a light and surveyed the painted rooms, talking herself out of walking back up the creek on some pretense to see him. The floors up here glistened in the light, the paint smell still strong even though she'd opened all the windows.

The faint breeze wafting in smelled of cotton-woods and summer nights. She stepped to it, breathing in the memories of her childhood summers. What kind of memories did the boys have who used to live here?

The thought startled her, just as did the creak of the stairs behind her. She spun around to find Nate Dempsey standing in the doorway.

NATE TRIED TO STILL the pounding in his pulse. He'd followed her up here with one thing in mind. But seeing her standing there…in this room…the summer smells coming through the open window—all of it took him back to a place he had never wanted to go again.

"You scared me," she snapped, a hand going to her heart, those blue eyes wide and frightened.

"I'm sorry. I didn't mean to startle you. I saw a light…." He was sick of the lying. "Are you all right?"

She nodded.

"I saw someone leaving the house," he said, trying not to let her see how upset he was.

"My *date*."

He couldn't miss her sarcasm. "I thought he'd take you back to your family ranch and you'd come over in the morning with your sisters. I didn't realize you'd be back here tonight."

"It *is* my house. I came back for my pickup."

He chewed on his cheek for a moment. She hadn't just come back for her truck. He suspected she'd come back to check up on him. And she wasn't just scared, she was angry. Angry with him.

"If I've done something to make you mad at me—"

"Other than scare me half to death?"

He sighed. "I apologize. I called up the stairs. I'm sorry you didn't hear me." Another lie.

She let out a long breath. "It's not you. It's me. I'm just tired." Lying seemed to be catching.

"So I take it your date didn't go well?" He hated how much that appealed to him.

"The date was fine. It's just been a long day and you scared me, that's all."

"Okay." He pretended to start back downstairs but hesitated as if as an afterthought. "Mind if I ask who that was you were with tonight?"

She touched her tongue to her lower lip, then seemed to make up her mind. Damn, but the woman had a fine mouth.

"Flynn Garrett."

Lucky was going by the name Flynn Garrett? Or maybe that was his *real* name, for all Nate knew. But why hadn't Lucky mentioned this? It took all of his self-control to keep from letting her see how upset he was.

"Flynn's the man I had dinner with the other night who I thought was my date." She frowned. "I thought you saw us together?"

A lie that had come back on him. When was he going to learn? "It was dark out front. I didn't recognize him. You're still seeing him?"

She cut her eyes to him.

"I'm not jealous, if that's what you're thinking."

"Why would I think that?"

"You can see anyone you want. It's just that… wasn't he at the auction? Didn't he bid against you?"

"What are you trying to say?" she asked, hands going to her hips, blue eyes firing.

"Nothing. I'm not trying to say anything. Just forget you even saw me tonight. I wouldn't want to ruin your *date*."

Since the first time he'd laid eyes on McKenna Bailey as a grown woman he'd done his damnedest not to notice just how much of a woman she'd become. But it had been getting next to impossible for some time now.

The thought of her with Lucky was enough to make him homicidal. Nate couldn't believe he was letting this woman work him up like this. What the hell was wrong with him?

And what the hell was Lucky up to?

Before Nate could descend the stairs, she grabbed his arm and spun him around to face her. "You have something to say, so let's hear it."

MCKENNA WASN'T ABOUT to let him get away that easily. He was angry and upset, and she wasn't going to just let him walk away until she knew what was going on with him. This had been coming for a long time between them, a tension building, and tonight was the night.

"Okay," he said slowly, squaring off against her. He seemed to choose his words carefully, although she could see that he was as angry as she'd been. "All I'm saying is that the guy might have ulterior motives, that's all. He bid against you on the house. He might think there's another way to get the house that would cost him even less if he plays his cards right."

As if she hadn't thought of that herself. "Unlike you," she said.

"I'm not after your *house.*"

"Oh, yeah? Then what *are* you after? I know you aren't out here out of the goodness of your heart— or for a place to board your horse. So why don't you be honest with me? Tell me the truth for once."

He took a step toward her, closing what little

distance there'd been between them, his brown eyes blazing. Suddenly there wasn't enough air in the room.

"You want honesty?" he asked, his voice deep and low and fired with passion. "You sure you can take it?"

She felt a hitch in her chest, but she held her ground.

"I *am* jealous, all right?" He was within inches of her now, his gaze locked with hers. "Ever since I first saw you, you've been a thorn in my side. I wanted you. I *wanted* to ride off with you. I still *want* you—and you're the last thing I need right now."

Before she could move or breathe or speak, his warm palm cupped her jaw and his mouth was on hers.

The kiss was even more unexpected in its effect on her. His free arm encircled her waist to drag her to him as he tipped her head back and deepened the kiss. She felt her toes curl, her face flush, her heart threaten to burst from her chest.

This was some kiss, and yet she suspected Nate Dempsey was just getting started.

She leaned into him, swallowed up in his embrace, in the feel of his mouth on hers, the taste of him. *She'd* wanted this. As crazy as it seemed, she'd dreamed of this from the day she'd first laid eyes on Nate Dempsey on the street in Whitehorse.

And just when she was being completely honest with herself about what she wanted from Nate Dempsey, he let her go.

"Any more questions?" he asked, his voice sounding rougher than sandpaper.

She shook her head, not trusting her voice. She was shaking all over and close to tears.

"I think that's enough honesty for one night, don't you?" he said.

*No! s*he thought. She couldn't stand to let him walk away. Not now. Her body cried out for him even as her mind warned her not to be a fool.

"Good night, McKenna. If you need me, you know where to find me."

With that, he turned and left, leaving her emotionally wasted, her body still tingling from his kiss and, worse, wanting more.

She stood for a long while listening to the thud of her heart before she went downstairs. She'd known he would be gone, but she'd half hoped he would come back.

Downstairs, she wandered through the house, telling herself she hadn't made a mistake. About this house. About Nate Dempsey.

But as she locked up and left, she feared she had on both counts.

NATE WAITED UNTIL McKenna left before he went to look for Lucky. He found him at the local bar.

At a glance, he could see that Lucky had had more than a few beers.

"We need to talk," Nate said, not bothering to take a stool.

Lucky grinned over at him. "Wondered how long it would be before you found out."

"Let's take this outside. *Now.*"

Lucky shoved away the half-empty bottle of beer sitting in front of him and slid off his stool. "Let's do it." He staggered a little as Nate let him lead the way outside.

The main street that ran through Whitehorse was nearly deserted except for the pickups parked in front of the bars. The night was dark and cool. A few streets over, a semi truck shifted down as it slowed to turn south off the Hi-Line highway.

"What the hell do you think you're doing going out with McKenna Bailey?" Nate demanded.

Lucky laughed. "Whoa, buddy. Look, McKenna and I had dinner together. When we ran into each other again I thought what the heck. But that was it. No chemistry, you know?"

Nate thought about the chemistry he felt around McKenna. "I don't want you seeing her again. It's too dangerous."

Lucky held up his hands. "You're telling me? Just picking her up at that house…it gave me the creeps."

"You sure you're up to what we had planned for tomorrow?" he asked.

Lucky straightened. "I'm sober as a judge."

Right.

"Hey, buddy," he said, laying a hand on Nate's shoulder. "You were my only friend at Harper House. I haven't forgotten that." His face seemed to cloud. "I just wish you could let this go, man. I really wish you could. I don't want anything bad to happen to you."

Nate nodded. "I appreciate that. So tomorrow morning, right?"

"Yeah," Lucky said, removing his hand and smiling ruefully. "Give me a couple hours. I'll do what I can."

Chapter Thirteen

The next morning when McKenna reached the house, she wasn't surprised to see that Nate's truck and horse trailer were gone.

And still her heart fell. Of course he would leave. He'd opened up to her last night. He'd told her how he felt and that she was the last thing he needed. And now he was gone.

She unlocked the front door to the house, hating the horrible ache she felt. What was it about this man? She was too smart to fall for someone like him. The man couldn't be any more unavailable. Was that the appeal?

Her furniture would be arriving this afternoon. Eve had called to say she had a wedding gown fitting so she and Faith wouldn't be out until afternoon to help.

Suddenly McKenna felt overwhelmed and had more doubts about her impetuousness in buying this house and starting a horse ranch. Had she been a fool to think that she could do this on her own? Let alone overcome this house's past?

At the sound of a vehicle, she saw Nate's pickup and horse trailer turn into the driveway. She hated the way her heart soared at just the sight of him. He hadn't left.

She frowned as she saw that he had two horses in the trailer. She hurried out to meet him. "Is that *my* horse?"

"I certainly hope so. Otherwise I'm going to be arrested and hanged as a horse thief." He looked shy and uncertain this morning. His hair sticking out from his Western straw hat looked still damp, as if he'd only recently come from a shower. She caught the fresh scent of him and felt an ache that went beyond wanting.

"Look," he was saying. "I hope you don't mind me taking it upon myself, but you've been working so hard on this place. I thought you might want to ride the property and remember maybe why you bought this place. It certainly couldn't have been because of the house."

She started to correct him but stopped herself. His offer couldn't have come at a better time. How did he know this was exactly what she needed? "Want to tell me how you knew which horse was mine?"

"I'm good, but I'm not so good that I just drove by your ranch and said, 'Hey, I bet McKenna

Bailey rides that paint.'" He smiled, his eyes warming her like the summer day. "I asked your sister Faith, told her what I had in mind, and she helped me load your mare in my trailer along with your saddle and tack."

Apparently Nate wasn't the only one who knew she needed her horse today. The thought of riding around the property instead of working on the house was more than a welcome one. She'd been so busy she hadn't ridden her horse in days. And riding with Nate…well, she couldn't have asked for anything better right now.

"Thank you," she said. A little voice at the back of her mind questioned his motive for the gesture, but she ignored it, refusing to look a gift horse in the mouth. Especially this particular one. "This was very thoughtful of you."

NATE SAID NOTHING, feeling the sting of guilt. Thoughtful was the last thing he was.

They saddled up and rode through the tall green grass undulating in the breeze. It was one of those days when the sky was as blue as McKenna's eyes. White clouds drifted along on the summer-scented breeze.

Nate loved days like this. He remembered hiding in the grass, staring up at such a sky and praying that someday he would escape Harper House. But his dream had been to learn to ride a horse and go riding with the girl he'd seen on the paint horse.

He glanced over at McKenna. As beautiful as the woman and the day were, it wasn't quite the dream he'd hoped for. In his dream he hadn't been doing it to get her away from the house for his own selfish reasons.

He pushed the thought away as they rode over a rise, the house disappearing behind them. They followed the edge of the creek to her property line, then angled toward a stand of juniper at the far corner.

In the distance he could make out the rough breaks of the Missouri River as it cut across this wild part of Montana. He was surprised how pretty this country was. He'd remembered it as stark, as stark as his heart had been when he'd finally escaped Harper House.

"If you tell anyone what happened here, no one will believe you," he'd been told by the people who'd run the place. "No one will want to adopt a child like that. They'll put you in a mental hospital behind bars, and you will never see daylight again."

At eight, he'd believed it. He'd known how powerless he was as a child. People believed adults, and he'd seen what these adults were capable of, as well as the other kids. He wasn't about to say a word.

"It's beautiful, isn't it?" McKenna said as she reined in her horse and sat looking out across the land.

"Yes." He wished he was seeing it for the first time. But in a way he was—through her eyes.

The breeze played at wisps of her blond hair that hung from beneath her straw hat. The hat was pushed back, exposing her sun-kissed face, the skin lightly freckled and glowing. She couldn't have been more beautiful. Or more unattainable.

He looked away, torn by a desire to have this woman that ran deeper than her roots in this untamed country.

"This would be a great spot to build a house," he said. From here, he couldn't see Harper House. From here, he could believe it no longer existed. Here, he could believe dreams came true.

"I *have* a house," she said, frowning over at him.

He wished he hadn't spoken and broken the spell. As she spurred her horse and took off down the slope toward a spot where the creek pooled, he caught a whiff of her perfume. It threatened to drop him to his knees.

By the time he caught up to her, she had already dismounted and was pulling off her boots.

He swung down from his horse and watched as she kicked aside her boots, stripped off her socks and rolled up her jeans to wade into the clear, flowing water.

She let out a squeal that made him laugh. "Aren't you going to join me?"

He knew the water would be ice-cold this time of year, but he couldn't resist the challenge he heard in her voice any more than he could resist the woman herself.

Shaking his head at his own foolhardiness, he tugged off his boots and socks and, rolling up his pant legs, waded in. "It's freezing cold!"

She laughed, a wonderful sound, and for a moment it could have been one of his boyhood dreams. They were kids on a summer day, playing in the creek. She splashed him, and he let out a shocked roar as the icy water took his breath away. He lunged for her as she splashed him again.

And time stopped. Their eyes locked across the frozen space. The suspended water droplets flashed in the summer sun and turned to jewels. Her laughter rode the breeze. And there it was: this connection between them that he'd fought ever since seeing the woman she'd become sitting astride that paint horse on the other side of the fence.

As he looked into her eyes he saw that she had felt it all those years ago, as well. Just as she felt it now.

Stunned at this realization, he couldn't help but feel all of this had been written in the stars years before they were to meet. As Lucky would say, it was fate.

He reached for her. Wet, her hand slipped his grip and she stumbled backward toward the deep pool. As she started to fall back into the deep water, he grabbed her again, but he only succeeded in going in with her.

The cold water took his breath away. Just as she did.

They both gasped as they surfaced. Her laughter filled the air and he pulled her into his arms.

Wet hair clung to her cheek. He brushed it back, his gaze going to her mouth an instant before his lips. The kiss was soft, tentative at first.

She wrapped her arms around his shoulders, gazing up at him, those blue eyes as challenging as they'd been only moments before.

He kissed her again, telling himself this was meant to be. And damned if it didn't feel that way.

"I'm freezing," she whispered against his lips.

He carried her over to the sunny green grass along the bank. Her fingers trembled as she tried to unbutton her shirt. He covered her hands with his and slowly unbuttoned the top button, then another. His gaze went to hers. She was watching him, those blue eyes no longer cool. Instead they burned like a hot, bright flame.

He freed the rest of the buttons to expose a pale lavender lace bra that did nothing to hide her hard, erect nipples.

His own desire was a pounding heat in his veins. He looked from her full, round breasts to her face as he slipped off her shirt and bent to touch his tongue to the dark nipple pressed tight against the lace fabric.

She moaned in response and reached to unbutton his shirt.

He stopped her. "You don't know me."

"Don't I?" she said.

Their gazes locked for a long moment, then he let go of her hands. She knew that boy he'd been. The one who still dreamed.

McKenna worked open the buttons on his shirt to spread the fabric aside. His chest was tanned and smooth, his abs hard and muscled, his shoulders broad and strong.

But as she rose on her knees to push the shirt from his shoulders, her finger brushed a scar. "My God," she breathed and leaned past him to stare at the network of scars laced across his back. "Who did this to you?"

He reached for his shirt.

"No." She moved back to face him, bending down to kiss his lips. He didn't yield at first.

She wrapped her arms around him, drawing him down on the grassy sun-drenched bank. She didn't question this need for this man. She'd never been this brazen. But then, she'd never felt this strongly about any man.

He drew back from her kiss, his eyes searching hers. Then slowly, his gaze still locked with hers, he began to unbutton her soaking wet jeans and free her from them. His fingertip trailed along the edge of her lace panties for a moment, his eyes taking her in as if memorizing every inch of her.

She'd always been shy with men. She'd only known two others intimately, one her high school sweetheart, the other a man she'd dated through most of college.

Neither had made her feel like this. But both of them had been "safe," men she'd known a long time. Nate Dempsey was neither. She didn't know him. Nor could she explain why he frightened her more than she wanted to admit. Just as she couldn't explain why she wanted him so fiercely.

As she began to unbutton his jeans, he reached behind her and unhooked her bra. She groaned as he freed her breasts and took one hard nipple in his mouth. Her body tingled at his touch, goose bumps rippling over her bare skin.

He worked off her panties as she did the same

with his jeans and shorts, and then they were both naked on the grassy creek bank, the breeze whispering in the trees over them, new leaves flickering, the light playing on their bodies as they made love. Once with a fever, then slowly, as if they might never get another chance.

"Do you want to tell me about it?" she asked as they lay spent on the creek bank. He'd left her only long enough to hang their clothing on a limb to dry in the sun. The horses grazed nearby to the murmur of the creek.

"No," Nate said and softened his words with a rueful smile. "It happened a long time ago."

She chewed thoughtfully, then asked where he'd learned to ride a horse.

He was thankful she hadn't pushed, as well as grateful that she'd brought up a pleasant memory. He told her about the ranch where he'd grown up in Paradise Valley along the Yellowstone River by Livingston.

"My adoptive family raised cattle and horses—quarter horses," he told her. "My adoptive father taught me how to ride. I fell in love with it immediately and I've had a horse ever since."

"What was your mother like?" she asked, not looking at him as she twisted a few strands of green grass in her fingers.

He knew what she was asking. "My birth

mother couldn't care for me. She was alone, and her choice in boyfriends left something to be desired." While avoiding the whole truth, he didn't lie to her. He couldn't. Not now. "I never knew my father. All I had of him was his name. I kept his name. Dempsey. It was all I had of my father. My adoptive parents understood. My birth mother had a lot of boyfriends, but she never remarried, even when she had my little brother years later. My adoptive mother was the most loving, generous woman I've ever known. She loved to bake. There were always cookies and pies and homemade ice cream. My adoptive parents more than made up for anything that had happened to me before they took me into their family."

"You must have made them proud," she said, finally meeting his gaze.

"I hope so." He glanced away, unable to shake the feeling that she knew. Not just why he was in Whitehorse but what he'd come here to do. "McKenna, don't move into the house. Not yet."

"Is that what this was about?" she demanded, sitting up abruptly.

"No, making love to you has nothing to do with—"

"Save your breath. I know it's never been about me. It's always been about whatever has you on this property."

"You're wrong. You have to understand it's about that man who came by—"

She was on her feet. "I thought you said he was gone."

"He'll be back."

"And you know that how? No, don't," she said, holding up her hands before he could speak. "I'm moving in. I don't need you to stay and *protect* me, if that's what you're worried about. I know that's not why you're here."

"Wait. I—"

"We should get back," she said, walking over to retrieve her clothing from the tree.

He rose, knowing that anything he said would be wrong. Too many people had told her that buying Harper House was a mistake. But it was her own doubts, he thought, that had her back up. She was determined to stick this out come hell or high water.

If he told her the truth—that the man who called himself Hal Turner was, he believed, in fact Roy Vaughn and a killer—then she would go to her future brother-in-law, the sheriff. And that would scare Vaughn away.

Nate couldn't let that happen. Once Roy Vaughn was dead…

But he knew it would be too late for him and McKenna. All the lies would come to the surface. And all the truths.

He avoided her gaze, wondering if he could feel any more guilty. He should never have let this happen.

As he dressed, his back to her, he cursed himself for forgetting what was at stake. And, more to the point, the danger.

Vaughn would be back. He could be watching them right now. If he thought for a moment that Nate cared for this woman…

Nate knew he'd have to fix this. In his attempt to keep McKenna safe, he'd only made matters worse.

He turned to look at her. She'd dressed and was now pulling on her boots, her eyes cast down. Did she regret what they'd done? How could she not?

What if she knew that while they'd been making love Lucky had been digging on the hillside behind her house for a body? And that this whole ride wasn't thoughtful but deceitful— just like Nate Dempsey himself.

Even if he told her how he felt about her…

He shoved that thought away. Any way he looked at it, this was going to have a bad end.

McKenna said nothing on the ride back to the house. Nor did Nate. What was there to say, anyway?

"If it's all right with you and Blue, I'll go ahead and keep my horse here, too," McKenna said as they unsaddled their horses. If anything, her words were a little cool. She acted as if she knew the score. They'd both gotten carried away. It had been consensual. No harm done. He should be grateful she was taking it so well. Instead he felt like hell and it was all he could do not to tell her how wrong she was.

"It was a nice break from working on the house," she said. "Thank you again."

He watched her turn and walk toward the house, head up, shoulders squared and back ramrod-straight. He cursed himself for hurting her.

"My pleasure," he whispered to himself as he watched her walk away. How much longer could he take being this close to her? He wanted her as desperately as he had back in the hills beside the creek. But then, he would always want this woman, he thought as she disappeared inside Harper House.

What he had to concentrate on was keeping her alive.

Chapter Fourteen

Nate had left shortly after their return from their horseback ride, and her sisters had arrived with a horse trailer full of her furniture.

Between painting and overseeing the placement of her things, the rest of the day passed in a haze. But not for one moment was Nate Dempsey far from her thoughts.

A mistake, her sister Eve' would have told her. And there were moments McKenna would have agreed. But she couldn't regret making love with him. Nate had opened up to her. Had she glimpsed the man she believed in her heart him to be?

He was such a mystery to her, and not for a moment was she foolish enough to think he wasn't hiding something from her. Holding back. She thought of the scars on his back. He'd implied that they had been the result of one of his birth mother's boyfriends. Not that it mattered who'd done it.

She thought about the boys who'd lived here at Harper House. Had they been just as cruelly treated?

"Are you all right?" Eve asked at her elbow.

McKenna came out of her thoughts with a start. "Fine."

"You seem a little flushed."

"I told you—I went on a horseback ride this morning. I guess I got too much sun."

Eve didn't look convinced. "Where is your hired man?"

"Nate? He's not my hired man."

Her sister was eyeing her intently. "Just be careful, okay? I don't want to see you get hurt."

McKenna started to deny that was a possibility but decided to save her breath. She nodded and felt tears burn her eyes. "Might be too late for that."

"I DIDN'T FIND A THING," Lucky said when Nate finally caught up with him late in the afternoon at the cabin he was staying in on Nelson Reservoir, outside of town. "I'm telling you there's nothing out there to find."

Nate walked over to the window to stare out at the water. He'd been upset since his horseback ride with McKenna. He hadn't been able to stop thinking about her. Or worrying about her safety.

He'd hoped that Lucky would find something. That he could quit sneaking around. Quit lying.

"Nate, come on, what if he left just like Roy said he did?"

"Johnny would have come back for me. He wouldn't have left me there," Nate said. He had to believe that. "He was my *brother.*"

"Maybe for some reason he couldn't come back for you before the state showed up."

"He would have found me somehow over the years."

"Not if he couldn't face you. Not if—"

Nate turned to look at him.

"Not if he ran out on you," Lucky finished. "Look, I know you don't want to hear this, but Johnny's body *isn't* out there. I dug in the area where you thought you saw Roy Vaughn bury someone that night. There's no body there."

"Then Vaughn got to it first."

"How is that possible? You were here within hours of hearing about Ellis Harper's death. You see any place where someone had been digging?"

Nate said nothing. Lucky was right. He couldn't explain what had happened to Johnny's body—just that he knew he was dead, that Johnny hadn't run away, that he had been buried late that night behind Harper House.

"I gotta tell you, I think you're wrong about Roy coming back, too," Lucky said. "After all this time, he's forgotten about the past. Hell, he could be dead."

"He's alive. A man calling himself Hal Turner turned up at Harper House."

"Hal Turner?"

"This man fits Roy's description—big, mean-looking."

Lucky laughed. "It's been more than twenty years. You're telling me that you can tell from that description that he's Roy? The last time you saw Roy Vaughn, he was *twelve.*"

"I'm telling you it's Vaughn. It has to be Vaughn."

Lucky shook his head. "If it's Vaughn and he's so hell-bent on revenge, then why are Frank Merkel and Rosemarie Blackmore still kickin'? And why aren't you dead? You've been making yourself a fine target ever since you hit town."

"You remember Vaughn. He liked to play games with our heads. He scared McKenna Bailey by showing up there twice, once pretending he was looking for a job, the second time by pushing her down as she was leaving the house."

Lucky blinked. "Giving her a push? Does that sound like *Roy* to you? He would just as soon cut her throat. Buddy, I think you're losing it here."

Nate hated to think how close Lucky was to the truth. "It has to end here. I'm not giving up on finding Johnny's body." Or taking down Roy Vaughn once and for all.

"Okay," he said, holding up his hands. "Then I'm with you."

"No, you've done enough. I don't want you involved. I never wanted you involved. Vaughn doesn't have anything against you." He started for the door, then stopped to look back at Lucky. "Let me handle this."

Lucky shook his head. "I don't know how you can do it, being out there. All the time I was digging behind the house I was looking over my shoulder—and it wasn't Roy Vaughn I was feeling behind me. It was all those memories, man."

"You *know* why I have to stay out there."

"Yeah? I'm telling you, you aren't going to find Johnny buried behind Harper House. He's tipping margaritas down in Florida with some hot woman in a bikini."

Nate wished that was the case. He could forgive Johnny for leaving. For running for his life. He wished with all his heart that's exactly what Johnny had done.

"It doesn't have to be this way. We can leave. Roy isn't coming back. None of them are coming back. It's over, don't you see? Even if you're right and Johnny *is* dead, nothing will bring him back. Roy ain't worth going to prison for the rest of your life."

Nate had no intention of going to prison. Vaughn would disappear. Just as Johnny had. "It won't be over for me until I find Johnny and his killer."

Lucky shook his head. "That's why I'm here."

"Thanks, but I'd feel better if you weren't around."

"No such luck, buddy. If you're determined to go through with this, then I am, too."

AFTER EVERYONE LEFT, McKenna finished unpacking a few more boxes. She knew she was just stalling, hoping to see Nate.

There was nothing stopping her from staying in the house tonight. She wouldn't need Nate Dempsey to protect her. When had she suddenly needed a man to protect her anyway?

When you bought this house.

It wasn't the house, she repeated silently to herself.

No, it's the house's past.

She could always sell the place and buy something else. She could send Nate packing.

But she knew she wouldn't do either.

"Why do you have to be so stubborn?" she asked aloud, her voice echoing in the room.

She wondered if her fight for this house was now more about stubbornness than the house itself.

And Nate Dempsey?

She knew how that would end. Heck, it probably already had. A man like him, one who'd built such a wall around himself, he would run as fast as he could after this. If his horse trailer wasn't still parked out back and his horse still in the pasture, she would have assumed he was already long gone.

At the sound of a vehicle, she went to the window. A truck slowed and turned in, the head-lights sweeping across the house. She ducked back until the lights passed the window before she looked out. Nate. Her heart took off at a gallop even as she tried to rein it in. *Don't go falling for this man.*

She watched him drive by, not slowing even though he had to see the lights on in the house and her pickup parked outside. She waited until she heard the truck engine die, knowing he wouldn't come to the house.

He didn't.

Disgusted with herself for even thinking that he would, she turned off the light and headed for her pickup, knowing she wouldn't get a wink of sleep here tonight. She'd deal with all this tomorrow. She wasn't in the habit of wanting unavailable men. She wasn't even in the habit of dating. She hadn't met anyone who interested her enough to date more than once for a long time now.

As for wantonly wanting a man as she had this morning on the bank of the creek…well, this was new territory and she felt completely inept at it.

It wasn't until she reached the truck that she realized something was wrong.

The yard light was out. Darkness and silence bathed the property, the nearby cottonwoods black against the sky. One tree cast a long, inky shadow over the pickup.

McKenna glanced toward the house as she fumbled her keys from her pocket. The night felt too quiet. Definitely too dark. This house far too isolated, even with her knowing that Nate was just down by the creek. It seemed too far away right now. A distance neither of them was willing to cross.

She started to open the pickup's door when her ankles were grabbed by someone hiding under her pickup. As her feet were jerked out from under her, she fell backward so fast she didn't have time to break her fall. Her back slammed into the ground, the air knocked from her. Before she could move, she heard him come clambering out from under the truck.

Instinctively she kicked at him as she fought to breathe, to scream, as she crab-walked furiously backward in an attempt to escape. But there was no getting away, no making a sound before his big hands grappled her to the ground and locked on her throat.

He bent over her, so close she could smell him and make out the coarse features of the man who called himself Hal Turner.

"Stupid bitch," he said as he tightened his

grip on her throat. "You should have cleared out when you had a chance."

NATE TOLD HIMSELF that going up to the house would be the worst thing he could do. The moment he saw McKenna he'd want her in his arms. He'd made that mistake earlier today. A man head over heels with a woman made mistakes.

He needed his mind on Roy Vaughn because he was betting that Roy's was on him. Worse, Nate worried that he'd already blown it. By morning McKenna Bailey would want him off her property. He was surprised she hadn't come out tonight to evict him.

Maybe she was pretending that what happened between them hadn't mattered. That she did this sort of thing all the time. But he knew better. She wasn't that kind of woman. She must be as upset about their lovemaking as he was. He just prayed it wasn't the worst mistake she would ever make. Because Vaughn had already been using her to get to Nate. If Vaughn thought that Nate cared anything about her…

He glanced toward the house before crawling into his tent. The lights were out. She'd probably left. He hadn't heard her drive away. Maybe she'd left as soon as he'd come in. Or maybe she was staying the night here.

Angry with himself, he lay on his back on his sleeping bag and listened to the night. Listened for the man who'd haunted his nightmares for years. He'd been so sure he would find Johnny's body. But then what? Without DNA tests, how could he even prove it was Johnny? And as for proof that Vaughn had killed him…

He swore. Why kid himself? He hadn't come here looking for justice. He'd planned to kill Vaughn in cold blood. He wanted revenge. Retribution. To hell with justice.

He also wanted to give his brother a proper burial. If he ever found his body.

Vaughn would know that he wasn't up here looking for evidence to convict Johnny's killer. He'd know that Nate was gunning for him. Is that why he hadn't shown?

Nate wasn't leaving here until Johnny's killer was dead. It surprised him that Lucky had tried to talk him into leaving without finishing this. Lucky wouldn't have been here if he hadn't known Nate, known exactly why he was here and what it would take to make him leave without what he'd come for.

The only thing Nate hadn't planned on was McKenna Bailey. He swore softly. Had he thought making love to her this morning would free him of the hold she had on him?

Well, that sure as hell hadn't happened. Just the

thought that he'd never be with McKenna Bailey again was killing him. He wished he'd never come back to this godforsaken place. Maybe Lucky was right. Maybe if he could just let it go—

He closed his eyes and quickly opened them again. If he closed his eyes, he feared he would hear the sounds he'd heard that night. The night Johnny disappeared. And the horrible silence that had followed. The silence had drawn him, then eight years old, to the back window under the eave.

He had leaned against the wall, afraid to look out as he'd heard the heavy tread of footsteps coming up the basement stairs, the thump of the back door, then the singing sound of the shovel blade digging into the rocks and soil in the backyard.

He had stood on tiptoe, turning to wipe the grime from the glass with shaking fingers before peering out into the darkness. He'd heard the wind. The tired scrape of a tree limb against the side of the house. The glass had trembled in its frame, and he'd shivered as the cold night air had crept in through the cracks.

At first he didn't see them, the fearful dark figures that moved in the night. But as the clouds had parted and the moon peered down on the hillside behind the house, he'd seen the hunched figures carrying something all wrapped up as if in a blanket.

He had buried his head under the covers as another ring of a shovel blade had filled the late-night air. He'd known one of the boys was dead. He'd just never dreamed it was Johnny, his own brother.

Inside the tent now, he heard the first scream.

THE HANDS ON HER throat loosened. McKenna got out one scream before the man closed his large hands around her neck again. She struggled to fight him off, but he was too heavy, too powerful. She swung wildly at him. But he only shook off her blows as if they were nothing more than pesky gnats.

She couldn't breathe. He was squeezing her throat, and the weight of him on her... All the time he was talking, but his words made no sense and he seemed to be distracted, as if he thought any moment Nate would appear to save her.

She stopped flailing at him. Air. She had to get air. Tiny black spots appeared on the edges of her vision. She had to get him off her or she was going to die.

Her hand dropped to the ground along the edge of the gravel driveway. Her fingers searched the grass and weeds, closing around something cold and heavy. A piece of rusted iron from the old iron fence. She grabbed it tightly in her fist, feeling as if she was about to pass out, and drove it into him.

He let out a bellow of surprise and pain. His hands released her to reach for the rusted iron now protruding from his chest. With one angry swipe, he jerked the rusted iron out and threw it into the darkness.

McKenna groped for something else to use for a weapon, realizing there would be nothing to stop him from killing her now.

She grabbed a small rock, swung it as hard as she could in the vicinity of the man's head as he reached again with both hands for her throat. A loud *whap* filled the air, then his startled angry cry.

Gulping air, she swung again, this time connecting with his forearm as he tried to grasp her arms. He howled with pain and lurched backward. She sat up, brandishing the rock gripped in her hand and scrambling away from him as she tried to get her feet under her.

She was woozy from lack of oxygen and disoriented. She sucked in more air, gasping, her throat on fire. He was getting to his feet, shaking his head like an angry bull and swearing.

She hurled the rock at him, hitting him in the chest. He let out a bellow as she clambered to her feet. He was between her and the pickup, so she turned and ran—not toward the house, because she knew she'd never be able to get inside and lock the door behind her before he caught up to her.

Instead she ran around the side of the house, headed for the creek and Nate, praying he would hear her cries for help, praying he hadn't gone for a horseback ride. She needed him as she'd never needed a man before.

She ran, screaming Nate's name, her legs aching, the breath in her lungs burning. She could hear the man behind her yelling something she couldn't make out. All she knew was that he was gaining on her.

His fingers dug into her shoulder and he pulled her down the way a lion takes down its prey.

She hit the ground hard.

"Scream, bitch, scream!" he yelled into her face.

Her chest heaved, her panic accelerating as she fought to catch her breath. She couldn't scream. She couldn't breathe again with him on top of her.

He slapped her, making her head snap to the side. Out of the corner of her eye she saw him ball up his fist and rear back to slug her. "I said scream."

She closed her eyes, anticipating the blow, knowing that it would be over soon. A boom filled the air, making her recoil as hot, wet spray splattered over her.

Her eyes flew open an instant before the man straddling her fell forward, his heavy, bloody body slumped across her, pinning her to the ground. A new surge of panic filled her as she felt his warm blood soaking into her clothing. She couldn't breathe, the weight of the man crushing her, the smell of his blood filling her nostrils.

"Get him off," she cried, shoving at the dead weight as Nate appeared, a gun gripped in both his hands, the barrel leveled at the man on top of her. "Get him off!"

Nate raised a foot, put his boot heel against the man's body and shoved, all the time keeping the gun on the man. The body flopped over into the weeds next to her with a soft thud—and a groan.

As she scrambled to her feet, she saw the cold fury on Nate's face as he crouched to put the gun to the man's temple.

"You sorry bastard," Nate said, bending over him.

She saw him saying something else to the man, but she wasn't close enough to hear. The man's eyes widened, though, and a terrible high-pitched laugh emanated from his mouth along with a stream of blood.

McKenna looked away, still trying to catch her breath, her throat in agony, her body trembling. When she looked back, the man on the ground was trying to say something.

He coughed, blood gurgling from his mouth, and spoke, his words coming out as if he was taking his last breath. She only caught a couple of words, but she saw Nate's expression.

Then the man's eyes rolled back in his head and he fell silent, leaving his last words floating in the night air.

McKenna stared, too stunned to move, to speak, as she watched Nate hurriedly check for a pulse. Apparently finding none, he holstered his gun and let out a string of curses.

"He said your name." Her words quaked like her body. "He *knew* you."

Chapter Fifteen

Nate froze, his back to her.

"I heard him," McKenna said, her voice rising. "He said, *Dempsey*. And it was you he was calling for when…" Her voice broke. "He wanted me to scream so *you* would come."

Nate closed his eyes for a moment. Hadn't he known it was just a matter of time?

"Who *are* you?" she asked behind him, sounding afraid—only this time of him.

He turned slowly to face her. They were only feet apart. A sliver of moon and a handful of stars illuminating the darkness around them. Her face was ghostly white and she was trembling, her shirt and jacket soaked dark with blood, her cheek scratched and her hands filthy and bleeding.

He wanted nothing more than to take her in his arms and hold her. To tell her everything was going to be all right. But he was tired of lying. And things were far from all right. "I'm a cop."

She shook her head and took a step back. "A cop who just happens to know a killer?"

None of that mattered. "Are you all right?" His voice sounded strange even to him. He'd gone from fear to a cold, steely rage that had always frightened him. He could see that his calmness at having just killed a man was scaring her as much as what she'd overheard.

"I asked you who you are," she snapped.

"I told you who I am," he said, stepping past her and heading toward his tent. There would be no comforting her right now. Nor was this the time to talk. Not that she would listen to what he had to tell her now anymore than she would later.

"Where do you think you're going?" she yelled after him.

"To call the sheriff," he said and kept walking. He wanted to comfort her, but he knew better than to even try. He could hear her behind him.

"You *knew* that man," she said to his back as she followed him at a distance to the tent.

He reached in and picked up his cell phone where he'd put it earlier, pressed 9-1-1 and only then did he turn to look at her.

"He said your *name*," she repeated.

"There's been a shooting at the old Harper place," he said into the phone when the operator answered. "A man's been killed. We need the sheriff." He looked at her in the sliver of moon that had broken free of the clouds and disconnected before the dispatcher could ask him any questions.

As he snapped the phone shut, he reached into his tent and grabbed his jacket, tossing it to her. He felt as shaken as she looked now that it was over.

He could see the bruises already forming on her neck—just as he'd seen that the bullet hole wasn't the only wound in the dead man's chest. She'd fought back and it had saved her life. He tried not to let himself think about what would have happened if he hadn't been here. But then she'd never have been attacked if he hadn't come back here.

"Tell me the truth," she said, glaring at him in the dim light as she angrily put on his jacket and crossed her arms over her chest.

The truth. What was that? "I think we should wait until the sheriff gets here. Here." He dragged his camp stool over to the ring of rocks he used for a fire pit. She didn't move. He could see that only stubbornness was holding her up. "Sit down before you fall down."

ALL THE FIGHT WENT out of her. Her legs seemed to crumble under her. Nate lunged for her, catching her around the waist to keep her from falling as he lowered her gently to the camp chair.

"The sheriff will be here soon," he said as he busied himself making a fire in the circle of rocks next to her.

She watched him, dazed and spent. A cop? He'd let her believe he owned a construction company. And a few minutes ago he'd acted like anything but a cop as he'd put his gun to that man's head. What had he whispered to him?

At first she'd thought Nate was scared for *her.* Angry for *her.* But after she'd heard the man say Nate's name and seen Nate's reaction when the man died, she'd known it had never been about her. Not Nate being at Harper House, nor this man showing up when he had.

Glancing back toward the house, she could make out the dark shape of the man lying dead in the weeds. She began to shake harder, soaked with the cold wetness of the man's blood beneath the jacket Nate had given her.

"You can't get out of those clothes until after the sheriff gets here," Nate said. "But the fire should help."

Why was he acting as if he cared? She stared down into the flames. As she listened to the crackle of the dry wood and watched the smoke rise into the night air, she tried not to relive the terror. Or look at Nate. Hadn't she known there was more to him being here?

Her eyes burned with tears. She squeezed them

shut, but still the hot tears leaked out and ran down her cheeks. She heard Nate move to her, crouch in front of her, felt the rough pads of his thumbs as he brushed at her tears. She tried to pull away but couldn't.

His arms came around her. She buried her face in his chest as in the distance she heard the wail of a siren growing closer and closer.

IT WAS LATE BY THE time the coroner and the ambulance pulled away from Harper House. The sheriff had taken their statements.

"This is the same man you said called himself Hal Turner?" Carter asked McKenna.

She only nodded since they'd already been over this a half dozen times.

"And you didn't think to tell me that he had tried to attack you?" the sheriff demanded.

"He didn't *attack* me. He pushed me. At least I think it was him. To tell you the truth, I thought I'd imagined it."

She'd told Carter everything she could remember from the moment the man grabbed her from under the pickup and knocked her down to stabbing him with the piece of rusty iron from the fence to running for her life only to be caught and almost killed before Nate shot the man.

The only thing she hadn't told him was her suspicions or what the man had said right before he died. She told herself she wasn't covering for Nate. She wouldn't do that. She knew she wasn't thinking clearly after everything she'd been through. She'd convinced herself that she couldn't be sure that the man had said Nate's name.

Dempsey.

She couldn't be sure she'd heard correctly since the rest of what the man had said made no sense. She could have misunderstood. Just as she'd misunderstood the man's motives last night? If she was right and he'd wanted her to scream so Nate would come…then the man must have had a death wish.

She had to talk to Nate alone. She wanted to know what was going on. Nate and the man *had* known each other. But what did that mean?

There was also a good chance that when Nate gave his statement he'd told the sheriff things he hadn't confided in her, since they'd given their statements separately.

Carter finally had one of the deputies drive her to the ranch so she could get a shower and change clothing. She was exhausted, but she knew she wouldn't be able to sleep. McKenna felt sick to her stomach. That was the first man she'd ever seen killed. She remembered the dead weight of him on her and shuddered.

Nate had been taken down to the sheriff's department for more questioning. Was it true Nate was a cop?

McKENNA HADN'T EXPECTED to get a wink of sleep even as exhausted as she'd been. So she was surprised when she'd awakened late the next morning.

She showered again, letting the water beat down on her until it ran cold, wishing she could wash away the memory of last night.

Humans are amazingly resilient. Except for a few aches and pains, she didn't feel any different. How was that possible when a man had tried to kill her, would have if Nate hadn't killed him? She tried not to think about how close she'd come to dying.

Even though the day was warm, she dressed in jeans and a long-sleeved shirt. Eve had thrown Nate's jacket he'd lent McKenna into the washer and dryer along with her own clothing. As she retrieved it, she was glad to see there were no bloodstains when each article of clothing came out of the dryer.

"Where do you think you're going?" Eve asked from the doorway. "After what you're been through, you should be in bed."

"I can't sleep and I can't just sit here. I have to know what's going on. I'm driving in to talk to

Carter." McKenna didn't mention that she was also going to find Nate.

Both Eve and Faith had gotten up when the deputy had brought her home late last night. No doubt Carter had called to inform them of what had happened. And yet they'd both quizzed her, one sitting on the closed toilet while the other perched on the edge of the tub as she took her shower.

"Carter isn't going to tell you anything if the killing is still under investigation," Eve said.

"The man died right in front of me." Right on top of her.

"After he tried to *kill* you. How's your throat, by the way?"

McKenna touched a finger to the bruises. "Sore, but I'll live."

Eve shook her head. "I don't want you going back to that house."

She knew better than to argue with her older sister right now. Eve had been terrified last night to hear about what had happened. Being older, and with the folks gone from the ranch, Eve felt responsible for her sisters' safety. It didn't matter that both Faith and McKenna were plenty old enough to take care of themselves. At least under normal circumstances.

"I'm just going into town. I'll be back as soon as I find out what's going on."

Eve eyed her. "Anita Samuelson called this morning. She said she has some photographs you had inquired about? She said she'd drop them off."

McKenna nodded. She'd completely forgotten she'd called the woman for the photos of Harper House. It seemed like a lifetime ago. Back when she'd been excited about the house.

"Are you sure you're all right?" Eve asked.

"I'm fine." It wasn't true and they both knew it. A person didn't get over something like this after a few hours sleep. Eve would have been even more worried if she'd known what had *really* kept McKenna awake.

SHERIFF CARTER JACKSON didn't seem at all surprised when McKenna walked into his office. He got to his feet and hurried around to offer her a chair.

"How are you?" he asked.

"Fine," she said automatically.

"I'm surprised Eve let you out of the house," he said, taking his chair again behind his desk.

"She knew she'd have to hog-tie me to keep me from coming to town to see you," McKenna said. "I need to know what you found out about the man."

Carter leaned back in his chair. "The investigation is ongoing at this p—"

"Eve told me you'd say that. Carter, please, I have to know."

He seemed to study her for a long moment. Finally, with a sigh, he said, "His prints came up with a hit. He served some time at Deer Lodge. His name is Dennis Jones."

She felt her heart rate shoot up. His name was on the list she'd found under the floorboards of the house. "Denny Jones."

Carter nodded. "He did spend some time at Harper House. Apparently the place was never state-certified, and some pretty awful things happened to the boys."

She sat back. "What about…"

"The blood oath, as you call it? I've contacted both Frank Merkel and Rosemarie Blackmore. They're both fine."

She knew she should have been relieved. "What if this Dennis Jones isn't the only one from Harper House in town?"

"This is why I didn't want to tell you," Carter said. "Jones hadn't made contact with either Frank or Rosemarie. The truth is, he recently escaped from a mental care facility where he was being treated for schizophrenia. His doctors believe he returned to Harper House because that was the part of his life he dwelled on most."

She shook her head, feeling as if she'd stepped into a nightmare and couldn't wake up. "What about Nate?"

"What about him?"

"He isn't being held for anything, is he? If he hadn't killed the man when he did…"

"No. He's free to leave."

To leave? "Is it true that he's a cop?"

Carter eyed her strangely. "He's on personal leave from the Paradise Police Department. You didn't know that?"

She hated to admit that she'd thought he owned a construction company until last night—when she'd seen him kill a man with a .38.

MCKENNA WAS ALMOST to the turnoff into Harper House when she saw Anita Samuelson's little white sedan pull into the yard ahead of her.

With a groan, McKenna turned into the driveway and parked beside the elderly woman's car.

Nate's pickup and horse trailer were parked out by the barn, but for how long? If she was right, Nate would be leaving town now. She couldn't shake the feeling that what had happened last night was why he'd stayed around. Why he'd finagled his way into staying near Harper House to begin with.

McKenna hoped to cut this short with Anita. The last thing on her mind was photographs of the house. But Anita was already getting out of her car, an old shoe box secured with a rubber band under one arm, her huge purse in the other.

"Perfect timing," Anita said as she headed for the porch. "I haven't had time to go through the photographs. I thought I would just let you see if there are any in here you can use of the house."

"Thank you," McKenna said, wishing the woman would just leave them and let her go through them later. But clearly that wasn't Anita's plan.

"I'd ask you in, but we're in the process of painting," McKenna said quickly. "Hardly any furniture, either."

"This will do fine," the older woman said as she lowered her bulk into one of the rockers McKenna's sisters had given her for a housewarming present.

"How are you doing today?" Anita asked once she'd settled in the rocker, one large hand lying protectively over the box of photos.

McKenna shot her a look. "You heard about last night?"

"Everyone in town knows. It must have been horrible. What did the man do to you?"

McKenna was glad that the shirt she wore covered most of the bruises on her neck. "He didn't get a chance to do anything before he was killed."

"Yes, by a police officer from Paradise."

McKenna shouldn't have been surprised, but she was stunned at how news moved on the Whitehorse grapevine. "Yes. That's why I don't have long to visit. I need to speak with the sheriff again."

"Oh?" Anita asked, all ears.

"You know he's marrying my sister Eve. He just worries about me being out here alone. In case the man hadn't been acting alone."

Anita suddenly glanced around, clearly nervous now.

"I'd better have a quick look at those photographs and get back into town," McKenna said.

Anita shoved the box at her.

McKenna slipped off the rubber band and opened the lid of the box. A dank, musty smell rose up from the snapshots. She'd thought there would be old photographs of the house that she might be able to enlarge and frame. It was an idea that had lost its luster after everything that had happened.

Her fingers began to shake as she saw a photograph sticking out of the box of three young boys standing in front of the house. Her heart thundered in her ears as she looked into their faces. She knew at once they had to be the boys who'd once lived in Harper House. The troubled boys that no one wanted.

For a moment she almost closed the box and handed it back to Anita, who was rocking nervously next to her. McKenna wasn't sure she could do this. She knew that seeing these boys in these photographs would only make her more invested in what had happened at this house. *Her* house.

"If this is a bad time, you could stop by my house one day—"

"No," McKenna said, and with her heart in her throat, began to leaf through the photographs.

There were old photographs of the Harpers intermixed with the others. Many of the photos were taken in the front yard of Harper House. Would it ever feel like it was hers? Or would it always belong to the boys and the horrible memories they had of the place?

The Harpers' own photographs resembled those of the boys. Grim faces, backs ramrod-straight, eyes narrowed. The Harpers hadn't been a cheerful bunch.

But the few photographs of the boys were heartbreakers. It was their expressions and what she saw in their eyes. A lack of hope.

In one shot she recognized a boy who could have been Dennis Jones. He was large and plain-faced, his expression hurt and angry.

She turned the photo over, hoping someone had written the name of the boy on the back. The back was blank.

In each snapshot the boys ranged from six or seven up to maybe eleven. They were dressed shabbily, hair uncut, faces appearing expressionless. But it was the eyes in some that made her draw back from them. She'd never seen such cold hatred in young boys' gazes.

She couldn't bear to look at any more. She scooped up the photographs, intending to tell Anita that she was going to have to take them to Carter at the sheriff's department. She couldn't bear the pain she saw in these boys' faces. Or her fear of what they had become as adults. She thought about Dennis Jones, that crazed look she'd seen in his eyes.

But as she was putting the photographs back into the shoe box, one of the boys' faces caught her eye. She froze.

The rest of the snapshots tumbled out of her hands and onto the porch floor. She'd seen that face—and that expression—before.

Her pulse boomed in her ears. He was the boy she'd seen all those years ago in the third-floor window. Her memory had been imperfect, but seeing the photograph and having seen him as an adult, she recognized him.

Now she knew why Nate Dempsey had looked so familiar. And why she'd thought Dennis Jones had said Nate's name.

The boys had both once lived in Harper House.

DENNY JONES. NATE HAD been so sure the man McKenna had described—the man who called himself Hal Turner—was Vaughn. Instead it was Jones?

Nate wondered if he wasn't wrong about everything else, as well. He was still shaken after last night. It wasn't every day that he killed a man, thank God.

Even when he'd seen that it was Denny instead of Roy Vaughn, Nate had been so sure that Vaughn had put him up to this. But Denny had been lost in the past. He'd been talking as if it were more than twenty years before and they were boys and telling anything you knew could get you killed.

The irony had cut Nate to the core. Denny had been dying and yet he'd refused to tell anything—even though Nate had always suspected Denny had been one of the boys who'd helped carry Johnny's body out to be buried.

The morning he awoke to learn that Johnny was gone, Nate didn't get a chance to talk to any of the other boys. The state had come and taken them away, most in separate cars to different destinations.

When he'd joined the police force in Paradise, Nate had tried to find out what had happened to some of the boys. Roy Vaughn in particular. But he'd come up empty. Roy had dropped off the radar. Just like Denny Jones.

Recently he'd discovered that Steven Cross,

Lyle Weston and Andrew Charles were dead. Bobby French was in prison. Nate had thought about paying him a visit. But Bobby had been in his bed that night at Harper House. So had Andrew Charles. The other boys had slept a floor below, in one of the large bedrooms next to the caretaker's room.

Nate rubbed his forehead. He hadn't gotten any sleep last night and it was starting to catch up with him. But how could he sleep? Right before Denny died, his mind seemed to clear and he'd said something that had rocked Nate to his core.

I saw Roy's soul leave his body. It drained off him like the blood that ran from his throat. I'm telling you the truth, Dempsey. The truth.

All McKenna had heard was the Dempsey part.

"Before he died," Nate had told the sheriff last night at Carter Jackson's office, "Jones said something about a man named Roy Vaughn." The moment Nate said it he saw the sheriff's expression.

"I got an APB this morning on Dennis Jones," Carter Jackson had told him. "Along with his escape from the mental facility, Jones was wanted for questioning in the death of one Roy Vaughn Martin."

So someone *had* adopted Roy. "He told me Vaughn's throat had been cut," Nate had said.

The sheriff had nodded. "The authorities found Jones's prints all over the murder scene, and there is an eyewitness who saw Jones leave Roy's after what sounded like an altercation. The neighbors had already called the police."

Nate had been thinking about Denny's last words. "He told me Vaughn's soul left his body just like his blood." No doubt on the way to hell. "I guess Jones was thinking his was about to do the same."

The sheriff had nodded. "Ravalli County is going to be glad to hear that Jones is dead. I would imagine it will help them tie up the loose ends in their murder cases."

"Murder *cases?*" Nate had asked.

"Roy had only recently gotten out of prison on a medical release," the sheriff had explained. "He was dying of cancer. He only had a short time to live. Are you thinking Roy got Dennis Jones out of the mental facility? If that is the case, then Jones probably did him a favor by cutting his throat."

Nate remembered the switchblade Vaughn had kept under his mattress at Harper House. Had Dennis Jones used Vaughn's own knife?

"Scares the hell out of me that he was after McKenna," the sheriff had said. "I'm glad you were there. We owe you a lot."

Nate had said nothing, having trouble fitting

into the hero role the sheriff was trying to put him in.

Since leaving the sheriff's office, he'd been trying to come to grips with the fact that Roy Vaughn was dead. He knew what was bothering him: he'd wanted to be the one who killed him. Instead he'd killed the man who'd taken that privilege from him. But if Vaughn had already been dying of cancer…

It wasn't supposed to end like this.

Or maybe it was, he thought, his thoughts going to McKenna, as they often did now.

For the first time Nate noticed that the wind had kicked up. The limbs of the cottonwoods slashed back and forth, groaning and creaking. In the distance he could see the black clouds of a storm coming this way and could almost smell the rain on the wind.

He looked toward the house and saw McKenna headed toward where he stood by the creek waiting for her. He'd heard her drive in earlier along with another car.

Her blond hair blew back from under her straw hat, her face in shadow. He watched her give a wide berth to where Dennis Jones had been killed the night before. The crime-scene tape had been taken down this morning after the sheriff had closed the investigation.

Nate knew that if he hadn't been a cop, it would

have taken a whole lot longer. Even if he was a cop on leave. When he'd asked for the personal leave after hearing about Ellis Harper's death, he hadn't planned to go back to Paradise, let alone to the police department. He thought he'd be a murderer, possibly on his way to Mexico. Or prison.

Now he wasn't sure what he was going to do.

As McKenna grew closer, he saw that she wore a pale blue checked shirt that brought out the same color blue in her eyes. The jeans hugged her slim body, the cowboy boots dusty from her walk out to him. He remembered every curve beneath her clothing, the pale soft skin, the tiny sprinkling of freckles, the feel and taste of her. It was all indelibly branded on his memory.

She raised her head, the wind whipping the ends of her hair, and he knew what was coming. It had been inevitable.

"I wasn't sure you'd still be here," she said, an edge to her voice.

"I wanted to see you before I left."

She raised a brow. "Were you finally going to tell me the truth about why you came here before you left?"

"No."

She nodded, anger sparking in all that blue. "I *know*. I know you used to live in Harper House. I know you were the boy who I saw in that third-floor window twenty-one years ago. I know you've been lying to me."

He hated the way she kept some distance between them. It reminded him of the way people had treated the Harper House boys when on the rare occasion they'd been taken into town. Fear, repulsion. And with her, anger. Was there regret there? Or just the anger?

"I should have told you," he said. "But then I knew what your reaction would be and I needed you to trust me so I could protect you."

"Protect me?" She shook her head angrily, raising her voice over the shriek of the wind. "You were waiting for that man to come back to kill him."

Not *that* man, but he didn't argue the point.

"You knew he'd come here," she said, eyes narrowing speculatively as she studied him. "Because of the pact you made as boys. Why wasn't your name on the list?"

"My brother and I refused to sign it," he said.

"Your *brother?* Let me guess—the one who owns a construction business in Park County?"

"The truck and construction company belong to my *younger* brother Robert. My mother had him after she farmed my older brother Johnny and me out to Harper House."

McKenna stopped, all her anger spent. How could she be angry with this man who had suffered so much at this house? The wind was screaming now and battering the cottonwood branches overhead. She felt the dark clouds moving in, but her mind was on nothing but the storm going on inside her.

"The scars on your back?" she asked.

"My mother's boyfriends. You should have seen my brother Johnny's back. He got it much worse for standing up for me."

She felt tears flood her eyes and bit her lip, forced herself to look away. Her hair blew into her face. She made a swipe at it as she looked at him again. "Why didn't you just tell me?"

He shook his head. "Harper House isn't something I tell *anyone* about. Especially someone who's just bought the place and plans to live there."

She stared at him, wondering how that would be possible now. "You mentioned your older brother Johnny. What happened to him?" she asked, recalling what he'd said about him and his older brother refusing to sign the revenge oath.

"Roy Vaughn killed him. He would have killed me, too, if the state people hadn't shown up the next morning when they did."

"Roy Vaughn?" She remembered the name from the list. She couldn't hide her shock. "You reported it, didn't you? And this Roy Vaughn went to prison."

"I told the state people, but they didn't believe me. Roy was twelve, older than most of us and bigger and stronger. He got the others to swear that my brother ran away the night before. The state never investigated. They had their hands full just trying to figure out what to do with us."

Her heart broke for him. "I'm so sorry."

He nodded, and she could tell the last thing he wanted was her sympathy.

"Your future brother-in-law told me last night that Vaughn's dead," Nate said. "It appears that Vaughn helped Dennis Jones escape from the mental facility, for whatever reason. Vaughn was dying of cancer and didn't have much time to live. Dennis apparently killed him before coming back to Harper House, presumably because the place still haunted him."

She thought about the digging behind the house and suddenly it all made sense. "You came back here to find your brother and kill the man who you believed murdered him."

He didn't answer, but she knew she was right.

"I take it you didn't find your brother's body," she said.

"No. Maybe Roy Vaughn moved it that night before the state came. I don't know."

She glanced back to where she remembered he'd been digging and frowned. The tall green grass undulated in the wind like ocean waves.

"Did you know there was a flood along the creek nine years ago?" she asked. "It washed out a part of that hillside and changed the course of the creek." She turned to point down the creek where a mound of dirt from the hillside had been deposited.

Nate swore as he stared down the creek to where she indicated, his face grim. "Would you mind if I did this alone?"

"You're going to get wet," she said, glancing up at the storm clouds, and realized how foolish that sounded. He wouldn't care about something as mundane as a rain shower.

She hesitated, wishing there was something more she could say, then she turned and ran against the wind back to the house. The sky overhead was black, the clouds ominous. She hadn't heard the weather report but suspected that a severe storm alert had gone out. In this part of Montana extremes in weather were common.

Back inside the house, she glanced out the window and saw Nate get the shovel from the barn and head down the creek. She turned away, unable to watch.

She wandered through the house. On the third floor, she stood at the window, the same one where she'd first laid eyes on Nate Dempsey. She tried not to think about what his life had been like here. Or his brother's. She prayed he would find his brother—and the peace she knew he so desperately needed.

Hugging herself, she looked around the room, seeing it through Nate's eyes. She'd told herself it was just a house made of inanimate objects that had no memory. No ability to hold on to the past. Or harbor evil.

But she knew this house would always remind her of the boys who'd lived here and suffered. It would always remind her of Nate.

How could *she* stay here?

She turned and caught movement from the front window. Moving to it, she saw a pickup pull into the driveway. She hadn't heard the engine, not with the sounds of the approaching storm. To her surprise, she recognized the truck and the man who threw open the door and raced through the wind toward the house.

What is Flynn Garrett doing here? she wondered as she headed downstairs.

Chapter Sixteen

Nate stared at the mound of dirt that the flood had deposited downstream. Grass and weeds grew lush green over the soil as if it had always been there. He hadn't even noticed it and would never have guessed part of the hillside had been washed down here.

He knew he was finally going to find his brother, and for a moment that knowledge made him incapable of action. He told himself that after all these years there might not be anything of his brother left. The flood or animals could have carried off his remains.

But Nate knew better. He told himself he was prepared for what he would find. This was no longer about revenge or justice or proving what had happened to his brother. This was now about burying Johnny. And moving on.

The earth was soft and damp here by the river as he turned his first bladeful of soil.

He thought about the woman in the house. Could McKenna Bailey move on after this? Would she keep the house? Sell the place? Hadn't she said she wanted to raise horses here? Paint horses. Like the one she'd been riding the very first time he saw her.

He stopped shoveling for a moment to look out across the rolling green hills, to imagine paint colts running in the wind across the green pasture. He wished she'd been able to complete her dream. He would have liked to have seen that here, he thought as he began to dig again.

The wind howled through the trees over his head, the cottonwood branches thrashing back and forth, freed leaves peppering him. The storm was imminent, the sky an odd color—the color it turned when it was about to hail.

He dug faster. The first raindrops lashed down, cold and hard. The rain dropped down through the trees, shredding the leaves over his head, running off the brim of his hat, soaking him to the skin.

He dug heedless of the storm, lost in the monotonous action until the blade of his shovel hit something with a thud. He bent down. What he'd struck seemed to be caught in some sort of fabric. How was that possible after all these years? But then he remembered. The quilts from the beds where they'd slept were made of old jeans that were said to wear like iron. Perfect for rough boys.

He pulled back the edge of the rotted material and saw what he knew was the leg bone of a boy of ten.

FROM THE WINDOW McKenna watched Flynn race toward the house as rain began to pour down on him. She hurried to open the front door, surprised to see him.

"What a storm," Flynn said as he shook the rain from his jacket before stepping inside. "I haven't seen anything like this in years." He stilled as he glanced around the living room, his expression turning grave.

The wind and rain beat against the old windows, making them rattle. She could no longer see the mailbox up on the road through the pouring rain and mist. All she could think about was Nate out in it.

"So are you here alone?" Flynn asked, drawing her attention away from the storm and Nate.

She felt a stab of unease at the odd question. "What?"

"Your sisters. I thought they would be here helping you paint or something."

She shook her head and watched Flynn look around the living room, his expression still grim.

Lightning flashed, and an instant later a boom

of thunder shook the house. McKenna jumped, surprised how tense she was.

"My mother was afraid of storms," Flynn said, noticing her reaction. "She always wanted me to sit with her. She would hold my hand and we would sing songs so she didn't have to listen to the thunder." He shook his head. "Funny the memories a storm brings back, huh?"

She nodded, wondering what he was doing here—and why he was making her so uneasy.

"So let's see the rest of the house," he said and headed toward the back without waiting for an answer. "It looks as if you're moving in." He started up the stairs.

She stood for a moment, then followed him. Obviously he'd just come out because he'd been worried about her after what had happened out here last night. And maybe he finally did want to see what she'd done with the house. After all, she had extended the invitation to him just the other day. She tried to relax, but the storm and worrying about Nate…

When she reached the third floor, she found Flynn standing at the window, looking toward the front of the house. "This was going to be my office," she said to his back.

"Was?" he asked, turning to face her.

"I don't think I'm staying in the house," she said and wished she hadn't said anything.

"Really?" He seemed almost amused by that. "What changed your mind?"

Nate. "Everything."

He nodded as he looked around the room. "They didn't come back," he said, his gaze lighting on her. "The boys. So much for that blood oath, huh?"

"One of them did. The one who…died out here last night."

"Yeah, I heard about that. I'm glad to see that you're all right. But wasn't he crazy or something?"

"I guess he'd been in a mental facility. Schizophrenia."

He nodded. "Well, all your worries were for nothing, it seems. I'm surprised, though, now that it's apparently over, why you aren't planning to stay. Wouldn't have anything to do with my buddy Nate Dempsey, would it?"

She felt a tremor of shock. "You know Nate?"

"Nate and I go way back. He knows me as Lucky, though. Lucky Thomas."

"You said your name was Flynn Garrett." McKenna felt as if her head was swimming.

"It is. Thomas Flynn Garrett. When Nate and I met here at Harper House, I called myself Lucky Thomas. Even at that young age I had a keen sense of irony. Lucky is the last thing I've ever been."

Lucky Thomas. She remembered his name on the list she'd found and felt her pulse begin to thrum. "You lived here?" Why hadn't he said something when she'd shown him the blood oath she'd found under the floorboards?

"I could tell you stories about this house that would make your hair curl." He frowned. "My mother liked that expression." He must have seen her face. "Don't look so panicked," he said with a laugh. "I didn't come back to Whitehorse because of the pact. I'm here because of Nate. I knew the minute I heard Ellis Harper had finally died what Nate would do."

She watched him move around the room as he talked and wished Nate would come in soon. Flynn bumped against a mirror she'd left leaning against the wall until she decided where to put it.

As the mirror fell over, he lunged for it with a curse. The glass hit the floor and shattered, making them both jump. Flynn began to swear, backing up from the broken mirror as if it were a rattlesnake coiled to strike.

"It's all right," she said quickly. "It was just an inexpensive mirror. Really, it's no big deal."

He turned on her, his eyes wide. "Seven years of bad luck. That's a pretty big deal."

"I don't think that really happens," she said cautiously.

He seemed to pull himself back together, but she noticed he avoided going near the mirror.

He was making her more nervous by the moment. Obviously something was bothering him. Between his odd behavior and the storm and what Nate was doing behind the house right now, she was a wreck.

"If you came out to see Nate—"

"He was like a brother to me." Flynn stopped again at the window, his back to her. "We didn't know each other for long, but I never forgot him. He was my best friend. My only friend in this house." Flynn turned to face her suddenly. "He saved my life when we were kids here. Did he tell you that? No," he said with a laugh before she could answer. "He wouldn't have mentioned me. But he told you he used to live here, didn't he?"

She nodded, unable to speak. She tried to assure herself that her fears weren't justified. Just because Flynn had been one of the boys in this house...

She glanced toward the window. The rain fell in a deluge, the wind gusts throwing it against the glass. By now Nate would have taken shelter. He couldn't still be digging. He would wait for the storm to let up before he came into the house. *If* he came to the house before he left.

"I owe Nate my life," Flynn was saying. "I would do anything to protect him. Hell, I already have. But I'm afraid it isn't going to be enough."

"I'm sure he's grateful for everything you've done for him."

Flynn laughed at that. "He doesn't even know the half of it. No one does."

Didn't he realize Nate was out back? Surely he would have seen Nate's pickup and horse trailer, unless he hadn't been able to see it through the rain.

He thought she was alone here. A shaft of icy fear raced up her spine. She was.

SHERIFF CARTER JACKSON picked up the APB that came over the wire just about the time the storm hit.

His second in command, Deputy Nick Giovanni, came in on a gust of wind and rain. "There's going to be some flooding for sure before this one's over."

"They're talking a chance for hail on the news." Storms like these always meant more accidents on the highways. He was glad Eve and Faith were at the ranch and not out in the middle of it. He recalled the last bad storm they'd had. Eve had been trapped in it.

Shoving that unpleasant thought away, he read the APB that had come in.

"Something up?" Nick asked.

"Double-murder suspect. He's driving a pickup with out-of-state plates. They think he might be in our area." Carter handed the information to Nick, who frowned.

"I think I've seen a truck like this in front of a cabin out on Nelson Reservoir," he said.

"He's wanted for questioning in the murder of a woman and her husband in Nebraska," Carter said. "Looked like an apparent robbery/murder. One of the neighbors had seen the pickup around for several weeks. It's believed he took money and credit cards. Could be a relative. One of the woman's former husbands was named Garrett."

"Wait a minute," Nick said as he saw the photograph being distributed. "I've *seen* this guy. He was at Northern Lights restaurant with McKenna the other night. I'm sure it's the same man."

Carter swore as he tried McKenna's cell first. She must have had it off, because it went straight to voice mail. He dialed the Bailey ranch.

Eve answered the phone.

"Hey," he said. "I'm hoping McKenna is there. I need to ask her a couple more questions."

"She left to go see you," Eve said.

"You don't know where else she might have gone?" he asked.

Eve groaned. "Probably back out to that house. You're sure everything is all right?"

"It will be once we're married," he said. "Got to go. I'll call you later." He got off the line before she could quiz him more. Eve had a way of seeing through most people, especially those she knew well. She could read him like a book.

"No luck?" Nick asked.

Carter shook his head as he reached for his hat and his patrol car keys. "You go out to the cabin where you saw his pickup. I'm going to find McKenna."

NATE SLUMPED DOWN into the mud as the rain washed the dirt from the bag of bones. Johnny.

He'd known Johnny wouldn't have left him to the cruelties of Harper House. Johnny had always protected him even though Johnny had always gotten the brunt of it.

Tears streamed down his face along with the rain as he turned his face up to the storm and let out a roar of rage, the sound lost in the wind. The storm was deafening, but it was nothing like the storm raging inside him. He felt powerless. He'd come back to find his brother and avenge his death.

But there would be no vengeance. Roy Vaughn was dead. So was Dennis Jones and whoever else had helped carry Johnny's body out to what would be a shallow, restless grave.

Nate drove his fist into the mud again and again as the storm thundered around him, the wind hurling stinging rain into his face, until his knuckles were bloody and bruised.

Johnny was dead. Just as Nate had known for years. But finding his body was more devastating than even he had imagined.

He wiped his jacket sleeve across his eyes and pushed himself to his feet again. Leaning down, he carefully pulled the bag of bones free of the mud. It was over. Roy Vaughn was dead. There would be no more looking over his shoulder. He would bury Johnny now. It was all he could do for the brother he'd loved more than life.

His fingers caught on something. He raised his hand, surprised to see that it was a thin silver chain. The end was hooked on the almost indistinguishable fabric of the old denim quilt.

He broke it loose and held the chain up to the light, letting the rain wash over the cheap chain that had tarnished from being in the ground and the small silver medallion that hung from it. This had been in with Johnny's body. Why?

He turned the medallion up to see it, wiping away the rest of the mud with his thumb, and saw with a start that it was a St. Christopher medal. His heart began to pound so erratically he didn't trust his legs. He slumped back against one of the cottonwood trunks. He'd only known one person who'd worn a St. Christopher medal.

My mother gave it to me, Nate remembered the boy saying. *It's the only thing I have from her.*

Even before Nate turned the medal over he knew what name would be there. Engraved into the silver was the word *Thomas.*

FLYNN MOVED TO THE back window. "I tried to convince Nate to let the past go. I did everything I could to protect him. But he just can't let it go, can he?"

"Maybe we should go see how he is," McKenna said. "He's just out back."

"Digging?" He stepped to the back window. "He's not going to find Johnny's body way down there."

McKenna's head snapped up, her pulse a thrum in her ears. Flynn seemed to have frozen, as if his own words had finally registered.

She glanced toward the doorway, but before she could take a step Flynn turned, and she saw what seemed to leap into his hand. She heard the snick of the switchblade as the blade shot out and saw the look on Flynn's handsome face as he blocked the doorway.

"No," she said, shaking her head as she stepped back, bumping into the wall. "I don't under-stand."

"I'm afraid you do," Flynn said.

She stared at the blade of the knife gleaming dully in the light from the storm. She feared she understood only too well as he came toward her.

The sound of a door slamming downstairs made them both turn. She opened her mouth, but Flynn was faster. He grabbed a handful of her hair and pressed the blade of the knife to her throat.

"You do exactly as I say and no one gets hurt," he whispered into her ear.

"McKenna?" Nate called from below them.

"Answer him," Flynn whispered. "Say *Up here, Nate.* And nothing more."

She felt the sting of the blade as Nate called her name again. "Don't come up!" she cried out. "He's got a knife!"

Flynn laughed. "So it's like that with you and Nate?" He shook his head at the sound of Nate's frantic footfalls on the stairs. "I guess we'll do it your way, then."

NATE STOPPED IN THE doorway, taking in everything in one quick flash: Lucky clutching a handful of McKenna's hair and holding a switchblade knife to her throat.

"Hello, Lucky," he said, feeling that cold calm come over him. "Or should I call you Flynn?"

"I like Flynn better since we both know that my luck has run out. You found Johnny?" He sounded surprised.

Nate nodded. "And I found this with his remains." He opened his hand and the St. Christopher medal tumbled out to dangle from the tarnished chain.

Flynn stared at it for a moment as if hypnotized, and Nate thought about rushing him but couldn't chance it. He met McKenna's gaze. She was scared but strong. He knew he could count on her when things hit the fan—which they were going to do. And soon.

"This is between you and me, Flynn," he said calmly. "Let McKenna go."

"I've tried to make up for what happened with Johnny," Flynn said, sounding close to tears.

"What *did* happen with Johnny?"

"You know how Johnny was. He wouldn't back down from Roy."

"I asked what happened the night you killed Johnny," Nate said.

"It was Roy. He made me do things." Flynn's voice trembled. "I knew he would hurt me if I didn't do what he said. I was just a *boy*," he wailed. "Didn't you ever wonder why Roy never hurt me? You had to know."

Nate knew. He'd never admitted it though, but it was one of the reasons he had hated Roy Vaughn for so many years.

"Then this one night Roy came over to my bed and told me I had to do something to prove my loyalty to him," Flynn said, pulling himself together. "If I didn't do it, he would kill you. I begged him, but Roy—" Flynn's voice broke.

"How did your St. Christopher medal end up with Johnny's body?"

"I put it there. It was all I had. I wanted to give Johnny something. Bad idea, huh?"

Nate nodded. Flynn had left a clue, one he must have realized later would come back to haunt him if Nate ever found his brother's remains. "So that's why you came up here the minute you heard Ellis Harper had died. Just like you said, you knew I'd be here looking for Johnny."

"I killed Roy for you," Flynn blurted out. "I heard he was living with his mother and her boy-friend. You should have seen Roy. He was dying of cancer and had wasted away to nothing. He cried like a baby when I killed him."

Nate felt sick. He could see the look of horror in McKenna's eyes. And the fear. She had to know just how dire this situation was. Did she also know that he would die trying to save her if it came to that?

McKenna watched Nate, afraid to do more than breathe. Flynn still had the blade to her throat. She knew he planned to kill her—just as he'd killed before.

It was Nate she didn't have a clue about. She'd seen that cold, calculated look on his face before, after he shot Dennis Jones. It frightened her even more now because she didn't have any idea what he was going to do faced with what he now knew.

"See, that's what's so crazy, Nate," Flynn was saying. "All of us spending years looking over our shoulders, worried about this bogeyman that no longer existed. It's whacked, man. Don't you see? It wasn't Roy we had to fear. It was the bogeyman inside us all. We took it with us when we left this house."

"No," Nate said.

"Bull. You came back here to kill Roy. What makes you any different from me? I tracked him down for you, man. I saved you from having to kill him."

"Only it turns out Roy wasn't responsible for Johnny's death. You were."

"How can you say that? I told you—Roy *made* me do it. You think I wanted to hurt Johnny? I knew how close you two were. I would have killed Dennis too, but he got away. I wasn't worried, though. I knew you could handle him."

"You got Dennis out," Nate said.

Flynn nodded. "I thought I was going to need some help with Roy. But as it turned out…"

"It's over," Nate said. "The cops know everything. You can't run far or fast enough. You need to turn yourself in," Nate said.

Flynn shook his head. McKenna could feel his agitation. "You know what would happen," he said, a whine to his voice. "Prison would be like Harper House. There would be another Roy

Vaughn. That's why it has to end here, in this house. I knew before I came back to Whitehorse that it would end like this. It's the only way I will ever find my peace. It's fate. *My* fate."

Something moved off to McKenna's left. Flynn didn't seem to notice as the black cat she'd seen before slipped into the room.

"Then let it end with just the two of us, like it was when we were boys," Nate said and took a step toward them.

"The two of us," Flynn repeated. "Just like old times, huh?" He shook his head and drew McKenna closer. The knife bit into her neck. She felt the sting and saw in Nate's eyes that Flynn had drawn blood.

"Sorry, Nate, but McKenna's the only one besides you and me who knows the truth. I can't let her go."

McKenna caught something in Nate's expression. He'd seen the black cat. She recalled how Flynn had reacted when he'd broken the mirror and met Nate's gaze. Did Nate know how superstitious Flynn was?

Suddenly the black cat came into view. It stopped in the middle of the room only feet from her and Flynn. She heard the sound that came out of Flynn when he saw the cat and knew this might be her only chance.

With both hands she shoved his arm away from her throat as she threw her body into him—and they both began to fall forward. Flynn let go of her hair as he fought to regain his balance, his gaze seemingly locked on the cat as they both went down. Out of the corner of her eye, she saw Nate spring toward them.

The cat let out a shriek, which was nearly drowned out by Flynn's cry of pain as the switchblade was twisted from his fingers.

She scrambled out of Flynn's grasp. As she turned she saw Flynn get to his feet. Nate was holding the switchblade. Time seemed to stop. The two men were staring across time at each other when the cat leaped up on the windowsill off to their right, drawing Nate's attention for just a second too long.

"Nate!" McKenna screamed as Flynn lunged for the knife.

But she saw at once that it had never been Flynn's intention to try to take the knife back. Flynn threw himself onto the blade, driving it deep into himself before Nate could move.

Flynn stumbled back. Blood bloomed across his shirt and over his fingers splayed over the wound. He glanced down at the blood, then up at Nate.

"I loved you like a brother, Nate. I could never have hurt you." Flynn started to fall forward.

Nate caught him and lowered him to the floor, and McKenna watched as Flynn died in Nate's arms.

Epilogue

A few days before her sister Eve's wedding, McKenna saddled her horse and rode out toward the Breaks. She hadn't ridden her horse since that day with Nate Dempsey.

It seemed a lifetime ago.

Nor had she been back to Harper House. Eve had insisted she stay at the ranch for a while, not make any big decisions until she'd given herself some time.

Nate had gone back to Paradise. Back to the police department. He'd called a few times. Just to see how she was. She always told him she was fine.

They didn't talk about Harper House. Or Flynn.

Carter had told her Flynn's history, about him being left at seven in a gas station bathroom on the edge of Whitehorse, and warned her that kids like that often couldn't get past their childhoods.

She knew what he was saying. Forget Nate Dempsey.

If only it was that easy.

She rode toward the wild country of the Breaks. It felt good to be back in a saddle. She'd missed riding. She told herself that she wouldn't think about Nate or Harper House, but of course that was impossible.

She hadn't gone far when she turned her horse and rode east. The barn came into view first, the horse weather vane on top moaning in the breeze. She slowed her horse as the house appeared out of the horizon.

She'd had a lot of time to think about the house—and why it had always called to her. While she wasn't superstitious, she wasn't so sure she didn't believe in fate. She'd seen Nate the first time in that house. And it had drawn her back years later.

If she hadn't bought the house, she knew her path and Nate's never would have crossed. She'd believed it was meant to be that she got the old Harper place. She still did.

But what about her happy ending? she asked herself as she rode up to the fence and sat staring at the house. She would never have it in Harper House.

While Eve had made her promise not to make any decisions until she'd given herself time, McKenna had made one she hadn't told anyone about.

Tomorrow the house would be razed. Eventually the land would heal—and maybe Nate would, too. By next spring the wild grasses would come back and all sign of Harper House would be gone.

No matter what she decided to do with the land, she couldn't let another unsuspecting soul move into that house.

She took one last look at the house and rode to the south until she reached the gate. Opening it, she rode across the pasture. Her pasture. How she had wanted to raise paint horses here. That dream was the hardest one to let go of. As Eve said, she could raise horses anywhere.

But that dream had always been connected to this place, McKenna realized. She didn't understand it, just knew it to be true. If she'd learned anything in all this, it was to trust and not question. Some things just were.

She reined in her horse at the top of the mountain, just as she and Nate had done. From this spot she couldn't see Harper House. From here the land stretched as far as the eye could see.

Her horse whinnied and moved under her. She hadn't heard the other rider. Blinded by the sun, she couldn't see him. But she recognized the horse. An Appaloosa.

Her heart leaped to her throat as Nate Dempsey rode up to join her. She stared at him, unable to utter more than a word. "How…?"

"Eve told me where to find you," he said as he looked out across the land as she had been doing only moments before.

She followed his gaze, her heart racing. For weeks she'd been trying to accept that Nate was gone. That he would never be back here. That the connection she'd felt between them hadn't existed.

"It's beautiful here," Nate said. "I never saw how beautiful until I saw it through your eyes. It would be a shame not to raise horses on this land, McKenna."

Tears welled in her eyes as she met his gaze.

"I think I mentioned that I thought here would be a great place for a house," he said. "I'm pretty good with a hammer, and you have a way with horses. I love you, McKenna. I loved you from the first time I saw you. So what do you say?"

What could she say as he dismounted and lifted her from her horse and into his arms?

His kiss was an early Fourth of July. The summer day was brighter than any she'd ever seen. And as he held her and they gazed out over the land, the future stretched before them, she knew that one day this place would be called "the old Dempsey place" and people would talk of all the paint horses that had been raised here.

McKenna knew as Nate bent to kiss her again that it would be their children and all the generations that would follow that would ultimately heal this place.

And it would be their love that would heal Nate Dempsey.

* * * * *

*Look for LAST WOLF WATCHING
by Rhyannon Byrd—
the exciting conclusion in the*
BLOODRUNNERS *miniseries
from Silhouette Nocturne.*

*Follow Michaela and Brody on their fierce
journey to find the truth and face the demons
from the past, as they reach the heart of the
battle between the Runners and the rogues.*

*Here is a sneak preview of book three,
LAST WOLF WATCHING.*

Michaela squinted, struggling to see through the impenetrable darkness. Everyone looked toward the Elders, but she knew Brody Carter still watched her. Michaela could feel the power of his gaze. Its heat. Its strength. And something that felt strangely like anger, though he had no reason to have any emotion toward her. Strangers from different worlds, brought together beneath the heavy silver moon on a night made for hell itself. That was their only connection.

The second she finished that thought, she knew it was a lie. But she couldn't deal with it now. Not tonight. Not when her whole world balanced on the edge of destruction.

Willing her backbone to keep her upright, Michaela Doucet focused on the towering blaze of a roaring bonfire that rose from the far side of the clearing, its orange flames burning with maniacal zeal against the inky black curtain of the night. Many of the Lycans had already shifted into their preternatural shapes, their fur-covered bodies standing like monstrous shadows at the edges of the forest as they waited with restless expectancy for her brother.

Her nineteen-year-old brother, Max, had been attacked by a rogue werewolf—a Lycan who preyed upon humans for food. Max had been bitten in the attack, which meant he was no longer human, but a breed of creature that existed between the two worlds of man and beast, much like the Bloodrunners themselves.

The Elders parted, and two hulking shapes emerged from the trees. In their wolf forms, the Lycans stood over seven feet tall, their legs bent at an odd angle as they stalked forward. They each held a thick chain that had been wound around their inside wrists, the twin lengths leading back into the shadows. The Lycans had taken no more than a few steps when they jerked on the chains, and her brother appeared.

Bound like an animal.

Biting at her trembling lower lip, she glanced left, then right, surprised to see that others had joined her. Now the Bloodrunners and their family and friends stood as a united force against the Silvercrest pack, which had yet to accept the fact that something sinister was eating away at its foundation—something that would rip down the protective walls that separated their world from the humans'. It occurred to Michaela that loyalties were being announced tonight—a separation made between those who would stand with the Runners in their fight against the rogues and those who blindly supported the pack's refusal to face reality. But all she could focus on was her brother. Max looked so hurt…so terrified.

"Leave him alone," she screamed, her soft-soled, black satin slip-ons struggling for purchase in the damp earth as she rushed toward Max, only to find herself lifted off the ground when a hard, heavily muscled arm clamped around her waist from behind, pulling her clear off her feet. "Damn it, let me down!" she snarled, unable to take her eyes off her brother as the golden-eyed Lycan kicked him.

Mindless with heartache and rage, Michaela clawed at the arm holding her, kicking her heels against whatever part of her captor's legs she could reach. "Stop it," a deep, husky voice grunted in her ear. "You're not helping him by losing it. I give you my word he'll survive the ceremony, but you have to keep it together."

"Nooooo!" she screamed, too hysterical to listen to reason. "You're monsters! All of you! Look what you've done to him! How dare you! *How dare you!*"

The arm tightened with a powerful flex of muscle, cinching her waist. Her breath sucked in on a sharp, wailing gasp.

"Shut up before you get both yourself and your brother killed. I will *not* let that happen. Do you understand me?" her captor growled, shaking her so hard that her teeth clicked together. "Do you understand me, Doucet?"

"Damn it," she cried, stricken as she watched one of the guards grab Max by his hair. Around them Lycans huffed and growled as they watched the spectacle, while others outright howled for the show to begin.

"That's enough!" the voice seethed in her ear. "They'll tear you apart before you even reach him, and I'll be damned if I'm going to stand here and watch you die."

Suddenly, through the haze of fear and agony and outrage in her mind, she finally recognized who'd caught her. *Brody*.

He held her in his arms, her body locked against his powerful form, her back to the burning heat of his chest. A low, keening sound of anguish tore through her, and her head dropped forward as hoarse sobs of pain ripped from her throat. "Let me go. I have to help him. *Please*," she begged brokenly, knowing only that she needed to get to Max. "Let me go, Brody."

He muttered something against her hair, his breath warm against her scalp, and Michaela could have sworn it was a single word…. But she must have heard wrong. She was too upset. Too furious. Too terrified. She must be out of her mind.

Because it sounded as if he'd quietly snarled the word *never*.

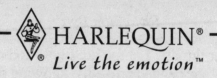

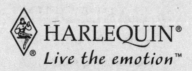

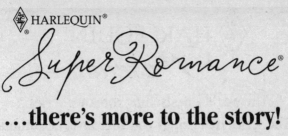

HARLEQUIN®
SuperRomance®

...there's more to the story!

Superromance.
A *big* satisfying read about unforgettable
characters. Each month we offer *six* very different
stories that range from family drama to adventure
and mystery, from highly emotional stories to
romantic comedies—and much more! Stories
about people you'll believe in and care about.
Stories too compelling to put down....

Our authors are among today's *best* romance
writers. You'll find familiar names and talented
newcomers. Many of them are award winners—
and you'll see why!

If you want the biggest and best
in romance fiction, you'll get it
from Superromance!

Exciting, Emotional, Unexpected...

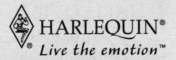

HARLEQUIN®
Live the emotion™

HARLEQUIN®
Presents

The world's bestselling romance series...
The series that brings you your favorite authors,
month after month:

Helen Bianchin...Emma Darcy
Lynne Graham...Penny Jordan
Miranda Lee...Sandra Marton
Anne Mather...Carole Mortimer
Susan Napier...Michelle Reid

and many more uniquely talented authors!

Wealthy, powerful, gorgeous men...
Women who have feelings just like your own...
The stories you love, set in exotic, glamorous locations...

HARLEQUIN®
Presents

Seduction and Passion Guaranteed!

Harlequin® Historical
Historical Romantic Adventure!

Imagine a time of chivalrous knights and unconventional ladies, roguish rakes and impetuous heiresses, rugged cowboys and spirited frontierswomen—these rich and vivid tales will capture your imagination!

Harlequin Historical… they're too good to miss!

HHDIR06

SPECIAL EDITION™

Emotional, compelling stories that capture the intensity of living, loving and creating a family in today's world.

Modern, passionate reads that are powerful and provocative.

nocturne

Dramatic and sensual tales of paranormal romance.

Romantic SUSPENSE

Romances that are sparked by danger and fueled by passion.